JOYCE'S GENE

Joyce's Gene

a novel

A. R. EGUIGUREN

Sun on Earth™ Books

Heathsville, Virginia

Published by Sun on Earth Books

www.sunonearth.com

Publisher's Cataloging-in-Publication Data
Eguiguren, A. R.
Joyce's Gene / A. R. Eguiguren. — 1st ed.
p. cm.
1. Genetics—Fiction.   2. James Joyce—Fiction.
3. Specialization—Fiction.   I. Title.
PS3555.G85J69 2005
813'.54—dc21   2004106891

ISBN 1-883378-45-1

PRINTED IN THE UNITED STATES OF AMERICA

Meanwhile, the past goes on handsomely...

— Andrew O'Hagan

one

Urine and water are half siblings.

One of life's major goals is to figure out which one you are.

Urine. Water.

The next step: accept what you are.

That done, simply count your blessings.

I met Gem and Professor Hewitt at the same time, though I didn't know it then. The three of us were wasting minutes, hours and days at *Café Le Clochard*.

It wasn't a real meeting. No introductions. I was staring at Gem from my table. And so was Hewitt, from his. Gem was at her own, writing.

I was there to write, too.

Failing to write.

Thinking: Others can do it. Why can't I?

I ordered a shot of whiskey with my coffee, and it didn't work.

I chain-smoked a pack every morning.

No luck. Just putting on an act. *Café Writer*. Sitting there with a pen. Hours of non-productive good intentions. Everything a waste.

Gem had no trouble with *her* act. She spent nearly all her time bent over a notebook, enjoying cigarettes like no one is allowed to enjoy them these days. A pure, benevolent drug. I was sure she was writing some sort of manual—instruction disguised as prose.

Every book worth its pulp is a life manual. Hemingway's *The Old Man and the Sea*'s real title is *How to Fish Like a Man*. His farewell to guns: *How to Fight Like a Man*. The Green Hills story: *How to Hunt Like a Man*. They're all how-to books, all manuals and instruction.

Le Clochard has kept up with the times. It serves frothy coffee and Internet access out back. Hardcore Hemingwayeans like us stick to the front—the old school of life. Booze. Cigars. Lots of sugar. Gem and I—at least we have that in common. No electronic gadgetry next to our MochaJavas.

Next to her notebook there's a test tube filled with an amber liquid. The tube is the diameter of her ring finger.

Her ring finger has no ring.

She writes as if taking dictation. No pauses. No writer's block. Makes it look so easy. Is the test tube a writing charm? Some authors need to have one with them while they write—lit candles, incense—to act as their muse.

Gem's beauty is balanced by teeth that are, slightly, on the large side, and by larger-than-average hands that any unkind observer would call manly.

Professor Hewitt has long hair. Gray and in a ponytail, but so thick, curly and luxurious, it seems unreal. The kind of hair many women would kill for.

I have nothing but whiskey, and my thoughts on what I'm going to do with my literary product. Everything humans generate is *product* these days. Perishable stuff that we better sell on market day or see it end up in the trash.

Sell what you write.

Write what's commercial.

Fistfights are more sellable than sex, say the how-to-write-a-bestseller books.

Sex is more popular than love.

Love is more popular than depression.

So, a likely commercial book: *How to Avoid Depression by Falling in Love That Leads to Sex & Fistfights*. Voted "Most Popular Title" by all literary journals. Purchased by a cable network to produce a talk show based on it.

High ratings. Big paychecks. Royalties. Freedom.

It could be me.

After the book's success, a television producer might think me talented enough to greet me in his office to discuss new ideas. "You have one minute to make your pitch," he'll say. "Start...now."

A minute. A sixtieth of an hourglass. A third of an egg timer.

I'm nervous. My next book/TV show is about spectacle, I tell him. Think RACE. A host and four guests on the show. Two ethnic-looking guests and two white ones. One of each race is a scholar. University professors, say. All four are ethnocentric to the core. Racists. Put them together. Give them a slide show. One slide: the scene of a holdup—a white man holding a gun aimed at a well-dressed ethnic woman clutching a leather purse. After each slide, the show's host asks each of the four guests to interpret the image. Totally open opinions. Use any words, express any thoughts. Violence allowed. There's only one condition to participate in the show: Be loud. Be *You*. Get rid of that heavy racial chip you got on your shoulder. Allow the audience to get rid of it, too, vicariously through the guests' own outbursts of violence. Let it all out. A disguised public-service announcement that lasts half an hour. *Feeling Racy?* How's that for a title?

The TV producer thanks me and says he'll let me know.

All the while, Gem goes on writing her masterpiece.

And Hewitt is there, too, at his own table, not even pretending to write but blatantly staring at her.

Gem doesn't know either one of us exists. Hewitt doesn't know I exist. I'm the only one who is aware of our triangle, our moment in time.

I don't like triangles of two men and one woman, especially when one of the men looks like a dirty old man.

There are moments in life when you meet someone by chance, someone who is about to die just a few minutes after you see them, and you have no idea of their impending demise. A minister, say, conducting a religious service in a retirement home. You are there, dusting the piano room. A bored employee. Your first day on the job. You see the minister leave and, for some strange reason, he waves at you. *Who are you?* he seems to be saying with his hand. Just the new janitor. The cleaner. But the minister waves at you. He's polite.

Then the news comes: Faulty red light. A truck that didn't stop. Providential intersection. The minister's gone. And you never met him except for that hand wave.

Hewitt doesn't look like a minister. But after seeing the way he stares at Gem, I would like him to become one.

Wave at me, Reverend. Wave as you leave the café. Let Providence turn this triangle into a straight line.

I left my parents at fifteen and never saw them again.

Haven't seen them again, I should say, since life is long and they're probably still out there somewhere, telling people what a promising young man I once was. There's a chance—one in a million?—that I will run into them again, someday.

In the meantime, I wait, thinking that if I let urine sit long enough, in the sun, it has a chance of becoming water.

Piss chance.

Urine has too many ingredients. Urea. Creatinine. Uric acid. Sodium chloride. Potassium. Calcium. Magnesium. Ammonia. Sulfate. Phosphate. Even the byproducts of human waste are a complex list of chemicals.

Once urine, always urine.

Why can't we accept that?

Aside from the long list of chemicals, humans are also cellular hourglasses. Instead of sand flowing through one hole, though, blood flows through millions of holes—our arteries and veins. In slow motion, blood drips through. The holes carry information, much like nerves do. If nerves are the hares of our bodies—the telecommunications network—our veins and arteries are the tortoises, pumping a mere 1.3 gallons per minute. They don't have to do anything, of course. They just sit there while the heart does all the work—2.4 ounces per heartbeat, 1,872 gallons a day.

When blood flows through the brain, its message is clear: *Engage in a gradual decline and deterioration.* And your cells are more than obedient. They follow the message to a T. They give you, the victim, enough time to suffer.

First comes the anger, then the paranoia. Stop and go. Then comes the verbal abuse. And the sexual incontinence. The drooling. The idiocy. While you wait.

Finally, adult diapers and raving madness.

Life is great.

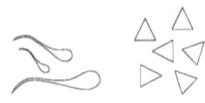

Today is my fourth week as a Research Associate at DataSearch. A longevity record in my recent career. I am as good at the job as a choirboy hitting high notes. I'll keep it for a few more weeks.

It's my evening job, so I can write in the morning. So I can sit at Le Clochard and waste my time staring at her.

There are at least a hundred other research associates on my floor. Cubicles. Computers. Telephones. The turnover is high.

Each associate is given a pile of resumes and job applications at the beginning of the shift. We create a file for each applicant and start the search.

If you've ever applied for a half-decent job, chances are your credentials have gone through a research associate at DataSearch. Even before the interview, your potential employer sends your boot-licking cover letter and resume to DataSearch. We call every one of your former employers: "Did applicant so-and-so ever work there?" we ask. Do the dates of employment match? Job duties? Accomplishments? Promotions? Anything else we should know?

The most important question is whether the former employer, based on his experience with the applicant, would hire the applicant again.

To avoid lawsuits, we have to ask the question that way. Most former employers answer with a simple Yes or No. But some don't care about lawsuits. "That son of a bitch," they tell me. "Fucked up *four* projects! Didn't know his ass from the coffee machine. Would I hire him again? I'll tell you."

And they tell me.

And I type every obscenity that comes out of their mouths describing the applicant. "Asshole." "Shithead." "Donkey-fucked moron!"

It's on the record, deep in DataSearch's servers and backup drives. *Asshole. Shithead. Donkey-fucked moron.* Next to the name of the applicant.

The resumes that receive the obscenity-laced recommendations get placed on a pile to the right of my computer. The *DataSearch Procedures Manual* commands us to label this pile "Excellent Prospects."

It's not an inside joke. Unlike certain former employers, the company is serious about lawsuits. Bad-apple applicants have to blame someone when months go by and they can't get a job. It's not going to be us.

And I have nothing to do with it.

Just my night job, my urine employment.

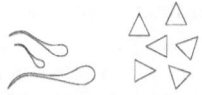

Today, there's no test tube next to Gem's ashtray, but she's still writing as if the presses were waiting for her manuscript.

No need for charms or talismans, after all. She's a natural.

She must have a rotten life. Comes here to unburden herself, and it all flows so easily.

That's my problem. I'm soft. My job's not miserable enough. There should be supervisors yelling at me all night. Computers crashing every five minutes. Irate clients calling with problems and letting me know what they think of my mother.

When it comes to writing, I'm stuck in Motel Mediocrity—a sleazy, middle-of-nowhere dump at the center of non-history. Born a couple of generations too late. If the 1890s had been my birth decade, instead of seventy years later, I would have lived through the Boxer Rebellion, World War I, II, the Bomb, Korea. I would have been a willing conscript in the Great War. There's nothing like an enemy to give meaning to your life.

Life as war. Suffer through cold nights. Rat-infested trenches. Corpses. Blood. Stench. Fear. Freedom.

When there's no meaning to your life, you look for it everywhere. You want to be everyone, exist in all places, learn everything.

You become a knowledge victim.

Le Clochard is just a short walk from *Real Companions*, a pet store that's almost a zoo. Customers can find any type of caged meat there, at a price. Pet snakes. Squirrels. Chinchillas.

I have an experiment in mind, but few animals appear suitable for it. The attendant asks me how much interaction I want to have with my new pet.

None.

She laughs. Pet-shop girls are a happy bunch. It takes a certain type of personality to work at one of these places. There's more to the job than talking to clueless customers and punching keys on the cash register. The critters have to be fed. And there is yesterday's paper lining the cages—heavy with pet urine—that needs to go out the door fast.

And mountains of shit. In little or big pellets. Creamy. Solid. Orangey. Black.

I worked here once. I know what this pet-shop girl does for a living.

"Do you sell mice?" I ask.

"Yes, white ones."

"Those the ones they use in labs?"

"I think so."

"Perfect."

She takes me to the Mouse Condo. Everything in the store is laid out as a city. Petville. Mice live in condos on Cheese Blvd. (a.k.a. Isle Four). Rabbits enjoy man-made warrens in the "Red-Light District," on Isle Six.

A useful mouse is one you can train. "Pet psychology is a current interest of mine," I tell her. "Have you ever heard of the book *How to Go Psycho With Pets?*"

She hasn't. It didn't make it to the bestseller lists, but there's useful information in it. Don't mind the catchy title. You know how publishers are. Anything to get attention. I want my pet to become a passive-aggressive mouse, trained to go for the kill when he runs into other mice in the house. There's a rodent problem inside the walls and my pantry. They sleep during the day and come out at night. Does she think a trained lab mouse could handle them?

She's never heard of such a thing. Can't tell. And there are no refunds or returns on purchased animals, sir.

All of a sudden I'm a Sir, just because my curiosity about the potential cognitive development of a rodent seems a little strange to her.

It's just an experiment, I tell her. Don't get upset. How can we learn more about life if we don't experiment?

Maybe a cat would be more useful. Less training to do. Less psychological meddling.

But a cat can't go inside walls.

I'll take the mouse, I say, and she seems crestfallen. A true pet-shop girl. Loves her job. Loves her animals. The prospect of some weirdo buying one of her mice makes her hands shake.

When I worked here, I was a much better employee. Always glad to see a customer leave the store with a new pet. One less beast to clean after.

Terminex. A fitting name for the mouse that will take care of my rodent problem. Terminex has to downscale from a condo on Cheese Boulevard to a cardboard box on my kitchen floor.

Sorry. A good hunter has to rough it to stay fit.

Don't expect any food, either. I don't eat, you don't eat.

I go on starvation walks every morning, before the regular people are out and about. There's no better hallucinogen than hunger. You go out for long walks. Skip one meal, two, three. By the fourth, your stomach doesn't ask for food anymore. It gets the picture.

Then your brain sets to work. Food is no longer important. Your cells go into slow-death mode. They understand that if they aren't fed again, they will eventually die. So every moment becomes a near-death experience. A vision.

You see your whole life pass by you, again and again. Then you see more: Other people's lives. Past. Present. Future. You are everyone and everything everywhere. You're one with time.

It's hard to go back to food after that, back to being one human being doing one job living one life. A Monomind. After three or four days of starvation walks, I know it's time to quit whatever job I have. Stop doing whatever I've been doing. Move on. Specialization is the result of not moving on. It's the drug of choice of the Monominds, and the enemy of us jacks of all trades.

The hungrier Terminex gets, the more aggressive. He'll tear through his cardboard condo. A Roman lion entering the arena of my pantry to deal with the food thieves.

Mice are territorial creatures. Put too many males in one place— inside a pantry, inside my walls—and there's bound to be blood. Their goal is to establish who's the leading macho mouse of the house. Who gets the females. Terminex. Gonad-bloated Terminex.

For Immediate Release: *Walls Oozing Blood After Amateur Psychologist Trains Mouse to Attack Kin.*

I have an email address book with 30,000 names in it. They all get an electronic news release every time I have something newsworthy to report.

Geneticist Patents Mighty Mouse.

Rodent Civil War: A Billion Dollar Industry.

At age ninety-two, I'm fantastically wealthy from my mouse-meddling empire. I am also wearing a diaper. My driver-cum-orderly takes me to the post office at nine every morning. He gets the mail while I wait in the idling Cadillac, thinking that, at some point, all the money must be spent. A fortune accumulated through a life of creative plundering and exploitation is worth nothing by the time you go back to wearing diapers.

At age thirty-eight, my permanent address is Le Clochard.

Profession: Failed writer, failed everything.

Civil Status: Metamorphosed. No wife. No children. Single-celled human. No Cadillac and no driver.

Gem hasn't brought her test tube to coffee hour again. It's just the memory of it that awakens my interest in biology. The how-to books say a good writer has to read before he can write. A novelist must study his subject.

Cliché: *Write what you know.*

If you don't know it, read about it. Do the research.

My plan is to write three major, fantastically lucrative books. The first one will actually be a series dealing with biology in everyday language. *Genetic Theory in 5 Minutes. Male Menopause in 5 Minutes. Cells in 5 Minutes.* The *5 Minutes* Biology Series.

DNA in 5 Minutes: "We all started as one-celled 'first animals.' All life forms on earth are related. The genetic code is identical for all forms of life. No matter how much you hate whomever, he's got *your* code. But the same genetic code does not mean reproduction between species."

If Gem and I can produce fertile offspring, it means we belong to the same species.

By contrast, a horse and a donkey can sleep together all they want, and they'll only give birth to sterile mules. Their genetic code is the same, but it contains enough spelling variations to discourage sexual relations between them. Same with human beings and their pet rodents. It just isn't done.

None of this is in the biology book I am using for research. Literary magazines always say that the best chapter in any book is the one you—the reader—add in your own mind as you read.

Chapter XYZ, Page 128: *On-and-Off Genes.*

Off, you're normal.

On, you're cancer patient 34,873 at Oncology, Inc. A team of millionaire doctors is having a blast trying to turn off your page-128 genes. Chemo & Rad. Cellular onslaught.

Because of all their highly specialized training, the poor doctors don't have a clue. Cancer genes are like three-way switches at both ends of a hallway. While the millionaires flip one off at one end, the cancer can easily turn itself on again at the other. And it does.

Chemo & Rad aren't very good electricians. Nor are millionaire doctors.

Hewitt is at his usual table. Coffee. Cigarette. His eyes fixed on Gem, as if he were trying to make me jealous on purpose.

The three of us could be in my pantry. And I could be Terminex. Hewitt a rival mouse trying to take over my territory. He's flipping my passion-aggression gene ON.

Last night, Terminex left for combat. His cardboard box was empty this morning. The only sign of rodent life in the kitchen: a mound of droppings on the lime-green counter. I expect to see him back tonight, white fur stiff with the dry blood of adversaries.

Getting rid of rodents with rodents. It's how dictators operate. The easiest path to power is to start a civil war. Rodent against rodent. It's all over the history books: Divide and conquer. You'd think smart citizens would have figured it out. But warmongering dictators...they keep on flipping switches on and off—at will. Smarter than doctors.

Hewitt looks like a smart man. Dictator material, with a twist.

Some women like ponytails in men. Does Gem? We'll never find out. She's totally oblivious, buried in her notes. Furiously writing. Why does she bother to come here at all? Anyone who can write like that doesn't need the café atmosphere for inspiration. She's just making the rest of us jealous.

You get the same feeling when you're struggling to write your stupid little book and there's best-selling author so-and-so, full of undeserved praise, showing up like clockwork in the Book section of the Sunday paper. He's the author of "the new best-selling book critics are calling better than sex!"

"Highly entertaining!!"

"A major triumph!"

Every six months, the same back-cover poseur posing again, giving you the finger: *I'm successful. I've been published, yet again! I'm productive. See my books sell. See me make money. Better than sex!*

Gem will end up as one of those.

And I'll stop reading the Sunday paper.

The jealousy gene.

On. Way on.

Page 134: How do you explain wisdom teeth and the useless appendix?

The Designer put them there. Man doesn't want them. Take them out because Darwin said we didn't need them anymore.

When a surgeon cuts them out, you can ask him to put them in a jar for you to take home. Souvenirs from the operating room. Useless molars that never had any food to crush. Hollow worm of the intestine that never processed anything until it tried to kill you. If you do take them home, make sure you keep them pickled.

And never ask a surgeon to give you your hernia to take home once he removes it. I made that mistake twice.

Hewitt is standing next to Gem, shaking her hand.

I press the Panic button, the switch, whatever. Turn him OFF.

But Hewitt is not a switch. And he's there, lingering next to Gem. And she's smiling at him. Her notebook to one side. Her pen down. Her hair gorgeous.

If it was going to be that easy, I could have done it. I would have approached her.

But I'm not one to approach people. And now I've missed my chance. And Hewitt and Gem...they're the same species.

TV show. Another pitch to the producer who never called me back on my first pitch. The network is probably producing the Race show already, behind my back. They changed the title slightly just so they can claim I had nothing to do with it. *Race Matters. Race Parade. Race it Was Our Idea and You Get no Royalties.* But I pitch again, and again, because you have to start somewhere.

My new show's host looks like an affable scientist. He may even wear a lab coat. Contestants must register by mail. With their application, they send in some of their hair, blood or saliva. Human DNA. Twenty amino acids for supercomputers to sequence. They sort all the genetic information into mega-databases in order to make a match.

Match Made in Heaven.

The Perfect Couple.

Then the man or the woman of this perfect-couple-to-be is invited to appear live, in front of a studio audience. He or she sits with the host on a stage. A hundred or so people of the opposite sex sit in the audience. One of those in the audience is his or her perfect match.

Say the contestant is a man. His DNA sweetheart is sitting among the hundred other participants. He's got to find her. It's a race towards love, romance, reproduction and marriage. Suspense that holds the TV audience through emergency-broadcast weather reports and loud commercials.

Our hero is given a set of questions to ask the studio audience. The hundred-or-so women answer by raising their hands.

Do you love to read?

Sixty-three young women raise their hands.

Mr. Lab-coated show host tells the thirty-four non-readers to leave the auditorium. They're out. Better luck next time.

Do you like hamburgers?

Hands go up.

Carnivores out.

And so on.

The DNA couple always ends up together. No need to rig the results. DNA matching is infallible, more accurate than meeting your future spouse on an Internet chat room.

Bye-bye, Divorce.

I start throwing titles for the show at the producer.

For Keeps. Fast Match. Till Death Do Us Part.

Made in Heaven. Made to Last.

I try to cover as many titles as possible so they can't come up with alternatives and cheat me out of my royalties.

Gene-Match. One+One. AminoCouple.

*D.N.A. = **Destiny Needs Alliance.***

The producer...he doesn't seem to bite. He's showing me the door.

Hand and Glove.

Out.

Sperm and Egg.

Out. Out. Out.

I'm sure he's just pretending. That's how television networks make their money. They rip off ideas from starving talent, from poor schmucks like me who don't have the resources to hire lawyers and fight fire with fire.

Reading Vegetarians, Unite!

Out.

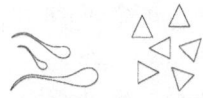

Gem and Hewitt leave the café together, and I don't see her again.

It's been weeks without her.

He comes, of course. All smiles and companionship. Shows up almost daily with a different woman.

Was Gem just his first victim? The one he needed to work up his nerve in order to start his serial-killing career?

That's how it all begins with them. One little taste of sexual violence and the switch is on. Can't stop killing, until they're caught and euthanized by order of The People.

Another option: He might just be a pimp, rewarding his workers with a cup of coffee every once in a while.

Or an S&M fiend, interviewing and trying out dominatrixes until he finds the right one. Pain without tissue damage. That's what he likes. Pleasure without consequences. *S&M Sans Frontiers.*

He comes. He goes. And I don't see any scars.

Now that Gem is not here, I should be writing. I have no excuse not to write. But with her table empty, I can see her better than ever. Her face up, not on her notebook. Her pale green eyes on me. Her extremely thin lips.

She's probably finished her book. A soon-to-be-successful non-fiction title. She's some biology expert. A specialist. A monomind.

I should have known. There are only two personality types: Monominds and Seekers. You talk to someone anywhere—at the supermarket, at the post office—for just two minutes, and you can tell right away what they are. Most everyone is a Mono. Only children are Seeks—human explorers taking in as much as they can before adulthood puts an end to their unbridled curiosity.

At the airport, a mother spreads a blanket on the floor and puts her baby on it. He explores everything with the intensity of a four-month-old. Arms forward. Head up. He turns this way and that. Blanket to mouth. Blanket abandoned. Toy to mouth. See how it tastes. I try to imitate him, staring for ten minutes at the pattern on my plaid shirt, as if encountering it for the first time in my life. Red. Black. Green. I imagine the boy analyzing the design, aware of the Scottish clan, regiment and district it identifies. Children know everything.

But forty years on, this kid will be a Mono. An accountant. Buried in numbers. No longer exploring. Brain dead.

Gem's not the only one who has disappeared.

Terminex has been gone long enough for me to consider him missing in action. Some soldier of fortune he turned out to be.

Money down the drain.

I still hear rodents raiding my pantry in the middle of the night.

I'm a frustrated general whose star soldier has failed him.

Frustration makes me pick up the pen.

Start a new book.

Start with the title.

The marketing of books is the marketing of titles. What's *in* the book doesn't really matter. Titles and covers make the sale.

Nation of Idiots: How Conservatives are Ruining Everything, Volume I.

A sure hit with liberals.

The idea is to insult as many readers as possible so that everyone will buy the book. Follow-up volume: *Liberalism: The Cancer of the Mind*. A runaway success with conservatives.

You have to cover the market.

For the younger crowd, only hip titles will do. *Suburban Chicks Do the Tango: Young Women in Charge of Powerful Men*.

Never forget the subtitle. It's the tease.

Also, for perennial worrywarts: *The Weather Tourist: How to Avoid Hail and Thunderstorms on Your Next Vacation*.

How to Steal Your Best Friend's Husband.

How to Legally Cheat on Your Taxes.

Writing self-help books is not much of a challenge. I need a more intricate contraption that will be as hard to write as it will be to read. A story of fictionalized, scholarly non-fiction. *Cerebral Fiction*, as they call it. Perfect for the young professionals who like to impress others with the books they buy but never read.

I finish my whiskey and come up with a title: *Locust of the Mind: the Postmodern Self-Actualization of Cognitive and Rational Individualism*.

Written by a specialist monomind, a fictional expert who knows absolutely everything there is to know about cognitive and rational individualism, whatever that may be.

Pen name: Dr. Reed Mendel Fixman, Ph.D.

That's our son, my parents would say. Their child the scientist. Not a successful lawyer, after all, but at least successful. An expert at *something*.

I write the Foreword by a made-up professional colleague, referring to me, the author, in full, informal pomposity: "What Reed is making reference to in this monumental work of scholarly science..."

One tablespoon of fantasized references.

Two cups of imagined sources and footnotes.

A pound of fictionalized bibliography, graphics and charts.

Stock photographs of unknowns identified as Professor so-and-so, Researcher this-and-that.

And finally, on the cover: "Translated from Esperanto by the Author."

Mock the publisher.

Mock the agents.

Send the thing around and laugh out loud when somebody buys it.

From the publisher: "Dear Dr. Fixman…We have received your manuscript. It's so bad…we definitely want to publish."

I start writing, furiously, like Gem, before I lose inspiration or gain enough clarity to consider the idea stupid.

The Introduction: *Humanity encompasses a vast array of cognitive and rational mental modes that humans, as neuron-oriented encephala-beings, must grapple with at one point or another in the course of their lives.*

Waiter, a coffee with rum, please.

And don't let me run out of cigarettes.

Civilization, and a rapidly advancing techno-Cartesian development wave of thought, has brought us, abruptly, to this point.

Footnote after "techno-Cartesian."

In this image of deity-infested atheism…

Hewitt is blocking my light.

His whore-dominatrix is next to him, too manicured to be any good with a whip.

"You a writer?" he asks.

I have to think. Every soul you meet changes your destiny.

Do I want to meet a serial-killer-S&M pimp?

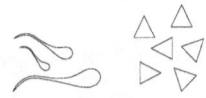

In biochemistry, a mutation is a change in DNA. To be inherited, the mutation must take place in the DNA of a reproductive cell, which can be found in the sperm and eggs of this world.

Microbiologists are eager to find a way to cause mutations in reproductive cells. Good mutations, of course. In the name of science and in the name of scholarship.

It's not playing God, they say. It's a quest for knowledge. You learn what you can in life—as much as you can. A quest for knowledge is the same as a quest to find God.

If there is a heart-attack gene in the reproductive cell, it has nothing to do with the heart itself. Instead, it allows fat to accumulate in the arteries that feed the heart. Once the arteries are blocked—Heart Attack.

Mutate the bad gene out of the reproductive cell, and you do away with heart disease.

That's the theory.

Byron A. Hewitt.

"Doctor," says his card. A business card not open for business. Just the name on it, and a phone number added under it, in pencil.

"Give me a call," Hewitt said. "I'm looking for writers."

I haven't called yet. He must have quite a collection of writers already. All women. All attractive. Like Gem.

A patient with the fat-collector gene will go to his doctor with chest pains. *Yes, it hurts, especially when I'm active.*

He'll go through the stress test to see how much blockage the gene has caused. (It's important to blame the gene and not the patient's diet or lifestyle.)

When you die of a heart attack and you're not famous, hardly anyone notices. Just one more victim of a bad diet and a trashy gene. Your loss is a private affair between you and your loved ones and whatever higher entity you believe in.

But die in a sensational plane crash, and everyone picks at your personal tragedy. Lists of passengers with their photos in every weekly magazine. Newlyweds such-and-such, on their way to their honeymoon. Or family of eight, attending a relative's funeral. And there you are, victim number 155. All the suffering becomes public, and there's nothing you can do about it. A nobody in life—"a forklift operator going for a week of fun in the sun"—with his fifteen minutes of fame after it's all over.

Hewitt is looking for writers. That's what I am, what I can be. Urine and water have nothing to do with our chosen professions. When it comes to those, we can be anything. Forklift operator. Scientist. Pilot of a doomed jetliner, or the flight attendant in love with that pilot. She survived because she had mono and was sick in bed on the day of the fateful flight.

Dr. Hewitt: *Give me a call.*

The beauty of it is that once you know whether you are urine or water, you are free to experience as many professions as your heart desires.

I am looking for writers.

Professional liquor-store sales clerk, where my job became a study of the customers who came in regularly, like clockwork, to get their fix. Friday. 7:55 p.m. Here comes Joe in his wool coat and hunting boots. Got your J&B right next to the register, Joe. For you, it's always on sale.

The same couple of migrant workers with their cement-covered hands counting the one hundred dollars in cash to play the same lottery numbers every week.

You a writer?

Maybe. But I have experience as a professional baker, working with mixers the size of bathtubs. I started each day at four in the morning, drawing a mythical bath. Yeast playing the role of Epson salts. Thick water of dough. The enzymes in the yeast turned the flour's starch into maltose, which the yeast turned into alcohol and carbon dioxide, which gassed up the dough. The alcohol evaporated during baking. That's why you can't get drunk on a loaf of bread.

My bakery boss, who had been in the business for thirty-four years, knew nothing of the beautiful chemistry of bread. He knew all the recipes and proportions by heart, of course. But he had never bothered to marvel about his tiny workers, the single-celled yeast fungi that did all the work. How can you be a baker all your life and not ask any questions about the little workers?

I started asking questions early in life.

Seeking answers from my father. Mostly at the dinner table.

How do they make tires, Dad?

How do they make silverware?

How do they make tablecloths?

Dad just sat there. Didn't know any of the answers.

Well, where did all this stuff *come* from, Dad?

"We just buy it at the store, Reed. Eat your fettuccini."

How do they make fettuccini?

The crave-a-new-profession-every-other-month gene.

I have it.

You a writer?

Of course. We're all writers, aren't we, Hewitt?

The heart specialist is telling you there's significant blockage in your coronary arteries. Something must be done.

Angioplasty. "It's a simple procedure," he says. The tool is inserted in one of your legs and guided, through the artery, to your chest, where it reaches the blockage near the heart.

Then comes the good part, the specialist says. "Think of a tight condom being stretched open by an erect penis."

He doesn't use the same analogy with women patients. But then, heart attacks are mostly for men.

"If arteries were endless condoms…"

Cardiologists can be poets, too.

Open up the artery so the blood can flow to the heart.

Got a bad gene? Deal with it through a medical procedure.

The anti-career gene is incurable, though. Symptoms: No steady job. No money. No ego.

Father warned me about it. He had the gene, too, but his parents took care of it. He wanted to become a dancer. They forced him to play a lawyer.

They encouraged him to marry at eighteen, to start a family and buy a house he couldn't afford. In the meantime, they paid for his law school. When he graduated, he was so tied down with wife, family and mortgage, he had no choice but to use his degree to get a job doing the only thing he was qualified to do.

The how-to-raise-your-children gene is inherited, too. *Do unto your offspring as your parents did unto you.*

My legal training began at age five: "Don't let the other boys at school push you around," Dad said. "Fight back. Tell your teacher on them." It was the elementary-school equivalent of filing a lawsuit, going to court, securing restraining orders, and collecting damages. By age ten, I was on my way to tobacco-company legal raids and lawyer-assisted golden parachutes for glass-ceilinged corporate minorities.

I found refuge in imaginary friends.

That was a problem. "Too much imagination, and the boy wants to become an artist." But the child psychologist told Mother that imaginary friends were a good thing. They help a child develop personality and self-confidence.

She wasn't reassured: "Too much personality and self-confidence, and the child becomes cocky. Cocky lawyers always end up as unsuccessful litigators, blacklisted by judges."

To curtail my imagination, I had to take daily naps. With the last bite of my lunch still in my mouth, Mother said, "Siesta time!" All cheerful and purposeful.

For Immediate Release: *Afternoon Naps Lead to Heart Attacks, New Study Proves.*

There's an inherent risk with angioplasty. When the balloon expands the artery, some of the fat that has accumulated there can break loose. A flake. A piece of danger that floats and flows on to the brain. When it gets there, it may once again block the flow of blood somewhere.

Stroke.

Heart attack of the brain.

Motor skills. Vision. Speech. Everything endangered.

"You're not taking a nap today," Mother said. "Your father...there was a problem with the *procedure*."

The condoms in his brain were too small.

We took him home in a wheelchair.

An abrupt change in roles: From man of the house to household pet. But unlike a pet, he required much more work from his masters, and less freedom. At least you can put a dog out in the yard when it gets on your nerves.

Mother became the man of the house. The strongman. I was no longer to marry at eighteen, produce several children and buy a large house. I was to hurry up growing up, and then lawyer my soul out to support her and whatever was left of Dad.

You a writer?

Yes, of course.

Hello? I'm looking for Byron A. Hewitt, doctor. Is he available?

The best time to learn microbiology is in your teens, when your hormones make your brain grow more and more interested in things sexual. Words like *zygote* and *mitosis* trigger fantasies that must end in after-school bouts of masturbation.

Zona pellucida. Impregnate. Venereal. Every subject of study has a few trigger words. *Concubinage. Prostitution. Vulva.* And a former civics professor's favorite: *Adultery.* "It's worse when a woman commits it," he used to teach, "because, if she gets pregnant, she brings *shame* to her household—somebody *else*'s child."

Hewitt doesn't shut up about microbiology. His religion.

We are having lunch at the *Authentic African*. The owner tells us she wanted her restaurant to be the real thing, the same as the one her parents had owned once in a small town in Tanzania. Plastic everywhere. Chairs. Plates. Cups. All made in China. Soft drinks served in warm bottles. French fries she calls "chips," and a stack of chapatis next to a plastic bowl of boiled ground beef swimming in salty water.

No more Le Clochard, Hewitt says. It's too open for our purposes. Here, there's privacy and noise. No one cares about our highly technical conversation.

Neither do I. I thought he was looking for writers, not scientists.

Hewitt says he retired early. But you never retire from being an inventor and entrepreneur. His most recent billion-dollar idea is now owned by the Pentagon, he says. The Spectrolfactometer. "You think you smell different after you've just taken a shower?" Smell again, he says. Each human being has a signature smell that never goes away.

Hewitt's invention can take a reading of your scent, translate it into a spectrum, digitize it, and store it in a database. The whole U.S. population will soon be odor-digitized, he says. No criminal will escape. Search dogs will become obsolete. Any smell can be bar-coded. Police officers will carry their hand-held electronic noses everywhere they go. A sort of breathalyzer for the whole spectrum of criminal activity.

But that was then, and here we are now. Patent sold to the military. Money in the bank. Chips and warmed-up orange soda on the table.

"I can't tell you what my new project's about yet," he says. "But I want you to be part of it."

It has to do with writing and art.

"Artists, you know, are la crème de la crème of civilization. If only they weren't so stupid about science, we'd be in much better shape."

Hewitt's ready to do something about it.

"The possibilities are endless," he says.

We go for a ten-minute, high-speed ride in his Jaguar.

"I'm *good* retired," he says. "Reaping the rewards of my inventions."

Crossing a bridge, I glance at the speedometer. Eighty miles an hour. I imagine a cop stopping us and sticking his digitizer up Hewitt's armpit.

Do you know you were doing eighty miles an hour, sir?

Deodorant won't save anyone a speeding ticket.

"When I was your age," Hewitt says, "I was still wasting my time trying to become a writer. I wrote three books and made nothing. Gave up that nonsense and went into the gene business instead. Sold it to a multi-national pharmaceutical company. That sale alone gave me the means to indulge in further scientific invention. You got any hobbies?"

"Crappy jobs. I collect them."

"You sound proud of it, too. But life without money's definitely not the ticket." Hewitt makes a sharp turn, then another.

"It's not about how much I earn," I say, "or how long I last flipping burgers, but how much knowledge comes to me from the experience."

"That's bullshit. You can learn a lot more when you have access to money."

Hewitt's house is four stories and a basement. High security walls. A long gravel driveway and landscaped gardens. "When the Authentic African becomes too dangerous," he says, "we'll start meeting here."

I don't ask.

He lives alone. Divorced. Framed photos of his children on the grand piano in the music room.

"I'm taking lessons," he says. "Being able to play music allows for a sense of superiority that few other activities can provide."

I can play, too. *A successful lawyer must know music and play at least the flute and the piano.*

The office next to the music room is four walls of books and what Hewitt calls his supercomputer. The machine sits alone on a conference table.

I take a seat in a padded leather chair. One of twenty.

He turns the forty-two-inch flat screen in my direction as it comes to life in bright tangerine.

"How old are you?" His hands on the keyboard.

Is this the interview? I take a few years off. "Thirty-two."

"Alright," he says. "Thirty-two thousand dollars. Let's try our luck."

With his long, thick hair, he looks like a successful business-woman at the peak of her game—too successful to bother with washing the gray out.

"The American stock markets are closed," he says. "But let's try Asia. If you know what you're doing, you can make thousands in just a few minutes, even if the markets are taking a dive. Tokyo is so-so. The Nikkei tends to be too Japanese. But who cares? For the more dynamic investor, there's always Bangkok, Singapore, even Manila. Let's spread the thirty-two-thou into an array of options, or puts—or whatever the market calls for. Ever had an authentic Cuban cigar?"

No. *Successful lawyers don't smoke.*

"Now's the time, then." Hewitt takes a book out from the shelf. A humidor shaped like a book. The spine reads *Mating Habits of the Potbellied Salamander.*

With the cigars throwing off smoke from our hands, Hewitt looks at the screen and says it's time to sell.

"Click here, and here…and here. Done! Just made fifty-eight hundred bucks. Not bad for a puny thirty-two-thou investment."

I'd like to know where Gem fits in all this.

"Who's your favorite author?" Hewitt asks.

I don't know. I don't have one.

"Come on. Every writer has a favorite writer. Not always the same one. They change through the years. But there's always a favorite of the moment."

"I don't read. I just write what I live."

Hewitt likes that. Says it's a good answer. "The best writing about wars comes from the soldiers who fought them. Down to earth. Full of grammatical mistakes. Real doughboy prose. Dead-man literature. Can you write like that?"

Maybe.

"Then give me a couple of months," he says, "and we're in business."

I don't get to ask what kind of business. The Jaguarous ride back to my dump is too fast to consider anything other than fatal luxury-car crashes. And that's all I see of Hewitt for a while.

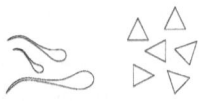

Every career change, no matter how frequent, requires some counseling. I go to Dr. Hurt's private practice, which he runs out of his house in a quiet residential neighborhood. He often opens the front door in his pajamas, then makes me wait in the study, where the walls are covered with prints of marine fantasies: Little men catching big fish. Harpoons that look like metal toothpicks.

Nothing ever changes in his office. The empty coffee mugs and half-smoked cigars are always there, half buried under piles of newsletters and magazines dealing with psychiatry and mental illness. Dr. Hurt never ages. The already thin, graying hair and wrinkled face are permanent features. He sits at his desk, still in his pajamas, and holds his very fat pen, filled with oceanic reservoirs of ink meant to last long writing sessions.

"Let's talk more about *Siesta Girl*," he says.

In elementary school, my classmates tormented me with that nickname. They didn't understand my parents' strategy—the idea that young children must sleep three hours every afternoon to develop a brain for good memory, a lawyer's memory.

Dr. Hurt loves the Siesta Girl story. He asks me to repeat it at least twice a year.

"After I was no longer a young child," I start, "they extended my afternoon naps to age ten, eleven, twelve. In my all-boys school, daily naps were for delicate girls. I was subjected to a barrage of *Siesta Girl, Siesta Girl, Siesta Girl!* Boys attended that school chiefly to practice their cruelty."

"Hold on," Dr. Hurt says. "You're going too fast." He takes notes furiously, filling out pages faster than Gem ever did at Le Clochard. "Alright. Continue with your tale."

"I withdrew. Feeling superior, of course. What did *they* do every afternoon? Watch cartoons? Homework? Eat peanut-butter-and-jelly sandwiches? I was not really sleeping, as my parents thought. The more time I spent in my bed, the more time I had to explore my sexuality. I was a man going to school with children."

"Good. Now tell me more about your friend."

"That was the added bonus," I say. "In bed, every afternoon, I created this imaginary lover—a childhood vice I called Siesta. A companion who hasn't let me down yet. She's not one of those toddler-sized pillows, filthy and in rags with years of use and abuse. I buy a new Siesta almost every year. When it gets too stained, out it goes."

"Many children have imaginary companions all through childhood," Dr. Hurt says. "Some carry them into adulthood. And that's fine. You just have to remember, if you have a Siesta in your life—and most of us do—you shouldn't tell anyone about her. Especially a job interviewer."

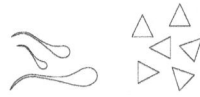

DataSearch evenings are still around, overstaying their welcome. If I get a late-night job as a janitor, I'll be able to get home exhausted. I'll also start rationing my food. Diet is crucial. Exhaustion and hunger—the best tools a writer can have. More useful than a dictionary, paper, typewriter, or even computer.

Bars are useful, too. Not so much for the booze but the atmosphere and material on which to base several novels' worth of shady characters, if you go to a bar in the right neighborhood. Off-duty janitors and mechanics and roofers playing pool. *Fuck*-everything language. Large pitchers of beer.

Women winking at you.

Men spitting.

Food frying.

Women winking at you.

How to Get Rid of Unwanted Female Attention. Chapter Six: "Tell them you're a hit man. Not the type who hits on women. Not that kind."

They're supposed to laugh, the book says.

"I bump people off for a living. There's a party at Reggio's tonight. Wanna go?"

They usually say No, and move on.

In the men's restroom there's a condom machine next to the urinal. The idea is that patrons read all the literature while they piss. A captive audience.

Fear-mongering decals with large purple words: *Syphilis. Gonorrhea. Herpes. HIV. Better have one of these condoms in your wallet! Don't risk infecting your sweetheart with your whore's business! Save your wife from nasty medical bills!*

Wife. Whore. Sweetheart. If the words imply female, they're in sharp contrast with the homosexual come-ons handwritten all over the wall.

Someone had the balls to write "I suck dick" in this busy bathroom. Bikers and construction workers come in and out every second to turn their beer into piss. No telling what reaction they might have if they caught some dick writing "I suck dick" on their walls.

So it must be the janitors. They work the bathrooms alone every night, when there's time to write urinal poetry undisturbed.

Dirty bathrooms. Filthy urinals. Shitty toilets.

Siesta says I need to get one of these bathroom-sanitation jobs, just for the experience. One more jack-of-all-trades project. Give it a try. Experience the brown coveralls with the name tag on the breast pocket. The polyester cap with *Worthwhile Sanitation Service* embroidered on it. *We Clean Toilets Like There's no Tomorrow!*

The job title is no longer Janitor but *Associate*. That's what it says on the tag under my name. *Reed. Associate.*

There are all sorts of public bathrooms to clean. In movie theaters. Airports. Office buildings. Restaurants and bars. The worst are bus and train stations.

Muriatic acid is an essential tool of the trade. Public-toilet porcelain turns brown quickly, especially under the rim. My new boss shows me his hand mirror. He puts it in the toilet to look up at the rim. I'm wearing my brand new uniform. Brown nylon pants. Striped shirt. A step up from coveralls.

"See that brown shit stuck to the rim?" he says. "That's a no-no." He teaches me how to *ream* the toilet. It sounds sexual, but it's nothing like that. Just pour a little muriatic acid on a scouring tool and ram the thing against the crevices and corners inside the toilet.

Ream. Ream. Ream.

Our employees must get rid of all encrusted mineral deposits.

The boss does spot checks with the mirror, he says. If he finds a toilet that hasn't been reamed properly on my route more than twice, I'm fired.

Mornings, I'm still working on *Locust of the Mind* at Le Clochard. It's going well, but what's the purpose? Fictionalized nonfiction doesn't transfer much knowledge. It doesn't share useful information the way how-to books do. How-to books are the bread and butter of knowledge activists—and the obsession of their knowledge victims.

Locust is as readable as a doctoral thesis. I'm piling it on as thick as I can, including some of the choice urinal literature I run into every night. I had to add a new chapter for the more scatological references: *Psycho-Rational Sexual Individualism.*

In the meantime, life goes on, one repetitive chore after another. The cave orangutans we're supposed to have devolved from were thinking animals, not meant for repetitive work. I can spend only so many days of my life cleaning toilets.

A genius—a Hewitt—would manufacture a tool or machine to do the toilet work for him. It's not money, but laziness—or the desire for leisure—that drives invention. It's our innate abhorrence of repetitive tasks.

We do something for a while, we learn as much as we can about it, and move on.

The first oranguhumans drank water from streams and found the drinking to be too much work. So they began to collect water in gourds.

Gourds were also too much work, so we settled down and dug wells. Then the gourds went into the wells with a rope.

Too boring. Way too repetitive.

So we invented hand pumps and windmills.

Then holding tanks. Electric pumps. Pressure tanks.

Plumbing.

Because the first oranguhumans couldn't stand repetitive activity—mouth to stream, mouth to stream, mouth to stream, mouth to stream—we get to draw water from faucets today.

Or from toilets.

There are hundreds of toilet designs to choose from. Some are very creative, with inside bottoms that look like the lips of a vulva. Somewhere, a toilet-design *Associate* had had enough of his job.

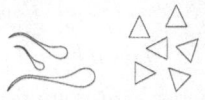

Deep into my 1,434th toilet, Hewitt throws me a bone.

Postcard from Paris.

"Every human life is a staircase to success," he writes in cursive. Then in tightly-packed print: "In the year 1632, a compound derivative of element number 21 on the Periodic Table was replaced with a synthetic compound that languished in obscurity for centuries, until it was picked up again in the early 1970s and used as an ingredient in a popular product that is sold to this day. What is that product's brand name?"

At the bottom of the postcard, in even finer print: "Password: *Boys-from-Brazil.*"

I order a large cup of coffee and go to the café's back room. Wait for a computer to become available and start the research with the most direct search string: "1632 periodic table synthetic ingredient popular." The search engine comes up with only one citation, which takes me to a blue page with large, red letters: "Enter the Password!" I do, and a new page says, "YOU'RE HIRED! Congratulations, Reed. I'll get back to you soon. —Hewitt."

Further research shows that Hewitt is also partial to fictionalized non-fiction. Scandium—number 21 on the Periodic Table—wasn't discovered until 1879. But the idea of a chemical fantasy appeals to me, and I can't resist sending an email news release to my growing list of media contacts:

> *Scandium, one of the trusted ingredients of mint-flavored toothpaste has been found to be highly carcinogenic in a controlled study of human subjects. Consumer groups across the country have organized to file a class-action lawsuit on behalf of toothpaste victims. The suit alleges that manufacturers knew all along that scandium was a cancer-causing ingredient. State attorneys general estimate a windfall for state coffers.*

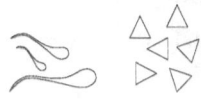

Siesta says it's time for me to earn more from my work. Abandon toilets and urinals. Embrace wool suits and cell phones.

Money-making requires a compromise, though: a full-time commitment to one employer, with Le Clochard and *Locust of the Mind* delegated to late evenings.

A temporary measure, we hope.

DataSearch allows someone like me to have access to a long list of well-paid openings. I know the employers. I know the applicants. No need to bother with the classifieds.

Search the database.

Enter how much I want to make.

Six figures.

Top consideration: Exorbitant salary. I search for positions that start with "Senior."

When I find what I like, I do a search for an applicant who has the qualifications for the job.

A Jonathan Preston comes up.

Perfect match. He's even close to me in age.

Mr. Preston's resume went through the system a few months ago. He got a job already. I print the resume and delete his record from the DataSearch server.

We never heard of him here.

I'm Jonathan Preston now, changing the color of my collar.

Every janitor should get to be a white-collar executive once in his life.

Senior Project Manager.

Dr. Hurt would say this is dishonesty—lying. But it's not. There's a big difference between lying and *experiencing.*

The company that has the job opening gets a packet from Data-Search. The envelope includes the list of candidates the company sent to DataSearch for vetting. Those who made it and those who didn't. Jonathan Preston's name is not one of the names they sent us, but it's listed among those who made it just the same. I enclose a copy of his resume, as well. The resume has my phone number and address on it.

If the company calls back saying, "What's this Mr. Preston's resume doing in the packet?" we tell them it's a mistake. Not in our system. Don't know how it got there. Please trash it.

Nine out of ten times, they don't complain. When they see that the interloping resume perfectly matches their position, they forget it wasn't supposed to be there in the first place.

Call Mr. Preston and arrange an interview right away. Time is of the essence.

Yes, sir.

The secretary dials my home number.

Everyone does this at DataSearch.

That's why the turnover's so high.

Everyone knows but our supervisor, who hasn't learned to get a better job with all the fabulous resources this place has to offer.

"Mr. Preston?"

Yes, this is he.

I can get a fake I.D. for thirty-five dollars. Mr. Preston. My face. My address. His Social Security number. My work. Let him get the retirement benefits. I'll only be a Senior Project Manager for a short while anyway.

Six-figure salary.

Seven, eight weeks of full-time employment. That would put me over $20,000 earned, more than enough to cover a year of writing first drafts at Le Clochard.

I wouldn't even have to bother with Hewitt.

Jonathan Preston. Harvard MBA. Intelligence officer—Gulf War.

I just have to prepare for the interview. Research the companies Preston worked for. Research the one that's doing the hiring. Learn the intricacies of every Preston job. Tell the interviewer, "Sorry, I can't talk about the war job. Still classified."

Speak with confidence.

Project the ability to boss people around.

And, as Dr. Hurt often says, "Remember that the person doing the interviewing is a human being, someone who once wore diapers and had to be potty trained, just like everyone else."

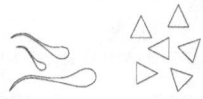

Postcard from Rome.

After a couple of lines filled with triple-superlative praises for my having found the scandium site...

One sentence: "Start reading up on genealogy."

No salary mentioned. No phone. No address or email.

The public library has more books on genealogy than public funding should permit.

Find Your Roots. A genre as popular as How-to-Lose-Weight paperbacks.

In the process of discovering your ancestral past—most of the books say—start with yourself:

My father was a...

I don't know what became of him.

His father was...

I never met him.

Father of the father was...

Blank.

And his father was...

A mystery.

As far as I know, no one was ever a writer in my family. No jacks of all trades, either. No learning victims.

But I have a theory: all ancestral lines lead to a jack of all trades—a JOAT. Heredity is like a savings account that no one ever touches. The interest earned on deposits makes the account grow with every generation. Whatever your great great great great grandmother learned in her lifetime is saved in that account—and the bank is your brain.

By the time you are born, the account is so full of knowledge that your head can't contain it. So you search for a way to make use of it by becoming a JOAT.

Part of this theory is not really mine. It goes back to a man of humble origins named Chevalier de Jean Baptiste Pierre Antoine de Monet Lamarck. He formulated his theory in 1809, in a then famous book titled *The Inheritance of Acquired Characteristics*. Hardly anyone knows of it today because, fifty years after it came out, another author, the former passenger of the *Beagle*, published a much more popular book: *On the Origin of Species*.

Best-selling author Darwin, back when naturalists were like movie stars, destroyed Lamarck's appeal. People loved their new matinee idol Darwin—the former medical student. He had abandoned medicine after being distressed by the screams from patients undergoing surgery without anesthetics.

Darwin was "seized by the ambition to make a mark as a man of science," his biographers say. He was not at all what modern-day Darwinists make him out to be. He was a man of God, and of a faith that evolved from pure orthodoxy to a flexibility "designed to catch falling Christians."

I'm in the middle of reading about the tragic death of Darwin's daughter when a new postcard arrives, from Dublin:

"Is there a gene somewhere in the human genome that *forces* its carrier to become a writer?" Signed, Byron A. H.

The answer will emerge from a simple database of writers.

I take liberties with Hewitt's question and expand it to include actors, singers, painters and others in the arts. "How many had children who couldn't escape their parents' professions?"

Dumas. Waugh. Amis.

Liza Minelli, with her Judy Garland gene.

Mia Farrow, with Maureen O'Sullivan chromosomes.

It's a fact that the offspring never match the greatness of their progenitors. They follow in their parents' footsteps mostly to entertain the entertainers. Sheen entertains the former Estevez. Jolie entertains Voight. Douglas entertains the onetime Danielovitch.

Genealogists are all about the obsession with last names, tracing back generations to an individual that is minimally related to us, but who counts just because of his last name.

In the thirteenth century, a third of the men in England were named John. They only used first names then, and it became a little confusing. *Hi, John. Hi, John. How ya doin', John. Have you seen John's son John, John?* Intellectuals were the first to put a stop to the nonsense by demanding the use of last names. John the pig farmer became John Bacon. John the iron worker became John Smith. John the pasture man became John Hayden. John the cobbler, John Shoemaker.

On a simplified pie chart, only fifty percent of our genetic material comes from our fathers, who most of the time get to give us our last names. Only a quarter of the genetic material comes from our fathers' fathers. And as we go further back, the genetic cocktail gets lost in oblivion. Thousands of historical beings have contributed to every human's genetic makeup. Still, the all-important last name gets most of the attention.

Last names don't mean much when Allen Konigsberg magically becomes Woody Allen, or Demetria Guynes turns into Demi Moore, Reggie Dwight into Elton John, Mark Vincent into Vin Diesel, and Alecia Moore into Pink.

You, too, can get a call from a lawyer someday—telling you that your last name is fake, that you're actually the illegitimate grandchild of a well-known billionaire, and the only legal heir. The billionaire's will asks that you submit to a DNA test. If you pass it, the fortune he left is yours.

Like winning the lottery.

Like landing a Senior Project Manager job at CUD Systems.

I haven't heard from them yet, but feel lucky enough to break the cardinal rule of job-hopping generalists: *Never quit a job before securing the next one.*

At three months, I had DataSearch seniority. They didn't want to lose me. Said I was so organized, punctual, respectful. Please stay.

They offered a raise.

It has nothing to do with the low salary and the poor working conditions, I told them. That's not why I quit.

**

Another postcard from Hewitt. Glasgow. Nothing on it but a crude drawing of a family with too many children. No return address, either. I'd like to know where to contact him, if only to ask him what happened to Gem.

In my days as a car dealer, credit limits on my collection of credit cards soared. I had nothing to do with the cars, just bought them for a friend using my plastic. One car after another. He'd buy in the morning and sell in the afternoon. Quick profits ranging from $5 to $200 per car, profits we split. He did all the work. I was the financier. The credit-card magician.

Buicks. Fords. The occasional beat-up Jaguar. I always had enough cash by the end of the month to pay the full credit balance. Credit card companies think you're a magnate when you charge so much and pay it all back in three or four weeks. They keep on increasing your cash-advance limits.

As a result, I can now deposit forty thousand dollars' worth of cash advances in an online brokerage account, and buy and sell stock with it. If Hewitt can do it, so can I.

Day trading requires no homework. You just go online half an hour before NASDAQ opens and read a few business headlines. Stick to news about flash-in-the-pan companies. With luck and good timing, they're the most lucrative.

As I browse, I take notes. Every investing step will go into some future bestseller I will manage to write when Siesta wants me to write it. A how-to book about online investing. *Latte & Security: How to Get Rich Quick at Your Local Internet Café Using Electrons and Plastic.* "Rule Number One: As soon as the market opens, buy stock from whatever companies have been mentioned in a positive light in the news. Number Two: Take note of those companies that have been badmouthed by the headlines and buy their stock the *fol-*

lowing morning, after it plunges. Three: Sell *everything* between eleven and one *every* afternoon."

If I make something, Siesta gets a new Winnie the Pooh pillowcase.

If I lose everything, it won't matter.

Here's the call:

"Mr. Preston?"

They want Mr. Preston to work for CUD Systems.

"Mr. Preston..."

Please, call me Jonathan. Happy to be part of the CUD Systems team. Lunch? Sure. Let's do lunch.

It's not so much what you know or what you learned at Harvard MBA, Inc. Employers don't care about that. The important thing is what the degree represents: That you can put up with monotony for years at a time. That you can stand lethal doses of monomind boredom. It's what they want—employees interested in only one thing: their jobs at CUD Systems. Nothing else.

Knowledge victims need not apply.

Poor dressers, don't bother.

With credit cards maxed out, I have to dip into my winning brokerage account to buy a few suits. Nothing but Brooks Brothers will do for CUD. One suit costs more than what I've spent in the last twenty years of thrift-store shopping.

But don't mind the expense, Senior Project Manager Preston. Six-figure salary man. Everything in life must be experienced at least once.

And I won't neglect my writing. CUD may not fit in with *Locust of the Mind*, but it will show up somewhere. There *is* a point in all this job-getting and quest for experience, after all. Let the cliché repeat itself one more time: *Write what you know.* And to know it, you first have to experience it.

How to Make a Cup of Coffee at Six in the Morning.
How to Successfully Brush Your Teeth.
Put every human activity between two covers.
Do it all, know it all.
How to Successfully Commute to Work.
How to Get the Most Out of One Roll of Toilet Paper.
How to Greet Everyone at Work Without Looking Like a Phony.
Write what you know.
Sell what you write.
Burn what you can't sell.
And start over.
Always over.

"When God is truly angry, even the fish drown." Session number 439, and Dr. Hurt is discussing hydrology. The wall behind him is covered with bloody Civil War scenes and portraits of Union soldiers.

"Tell me about your writing," he says. "Is it flowing at all?"

He knows the answer. Every one of our sessions includes a long discussion about the human capacity for literary output. "The average writer," he always says, "who writes perhaps twenty to forty books in a lifetime, produces, in fact, hundreds. Most of them are only in his mind and simply never get written. The ideas come, one after another, and then disappear before ever getting committed to paper."

As if to show me what he means, he picks up a notepad and pen. "Tell me what stories have come to mind. Let me help you get started."

I search for recent ideas. "One has to do with mental travel. The title is *Backyard.* The main character—Fern—lives in an old house with a large backyard connected to some woods. Fern used to go on trips everywhere—Europe, Asia—and hike several miles every day. But now, the only place she can go to is her backyard, so she goes there, daily. Spends several hours walking, first in loops around the backyard, then in the woods. The story deals with the geography of mental tourism. It covers philosophy, fauna, and what Fern has to pack in the large backpack she carries. There's a map of her back-yard to go with the story, and..."

"Stop! That story's going nowhere." Dr. Hurt lifts his pen from the paper. "Leave those philosophical ruminations for when we're talking psychology. Tell me a good yarn here."

"I have hundreds, Dr. Hurt."

"Good, good. Just pitch them to me, as if you were pitching a television show to a producer."

"Can we talk about a dream I had now?"

Dr. Hurt doesn't care about dreams. Says they aren't fictional enough.

But I insist: "The dream has me arriving at some international airport where everyone speaks a language I don't know. The place is so crowded that going through customs turns into an ordeal that never ends. Constant questioning. Constant suspicion. 'What's in your bag?!!' they ask, one official after another, as we passengers go through a gauntlet. When I finally make it outside, I'm assailed by touts posing as taxi drivers. I turn them all down. There's a huge billboard right next to the terminal. It says, *You're HERE! Now What?*"

"That's useful," Dr. Hurt says, "but let's go back to literary output here. Next story idea, please."

"I have one titled *The Nasty Obituarist*, about a woman who's hired to write final smear jobs on her clients' enemies. Character assassinations even after the characters are dead. She does her work very subtly, expertly hiding insult with words like, *Mr. Smith was held in the highest regard by a number of defrocked politicians...*"

"Stop! Next, please."

"A spiritual man who develops an endless source of electricity contained in a small box called the PowerBox. He manufactures billions of the boxes and practically gives them away. He wants the poorest of the poorest to be able to afford electricity. Each box, however, has a sort of spiritual password, so that it can only work for people who are spiritually true—individuals whom the inventor of the box calls *Trues*. In a matter of months, it becomes clear, everywhere in the world, who is a True and who is not. The miracle of electricity glows from the homes of all Trues on earth, while the Untrues live in the cold and darkness. With the invention of the PowerBox, utility companies cease to produce electricity, so the only way to get power is from a PowerBox."

"Good little story, Reed. Next pitch."

"Trite Vietnam War tale about a veteran who forces himself to go back to modern Vietnam to deal with his past. A form of therapy he uses to get over the trauma of a lifetime."

"Wait a moment." Dr. Hurt can hardly run his pen fast enough to put all the words on paper. "And let's say this Vietnam veteran...he left a local girl pregnant during the war, and now the child is grown, and maybe the boy-now-a-man hates his father, but he also has to force himself to deal with him as his *own* form of therapy!"

"Yes, Dr. Hurt. Whatever."

"*Papa Sam!* How's that for a title?!"

Dr. Hurt is often more excited about my never-written stories than I will ever be. He can visualize them with much more vitality and color. He can fantasize about being a successful author, while I merely try and fail. Fantasy always trumps effort.

"Papa Sam arrives in old Saigon, and..."

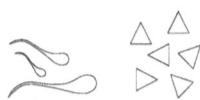

There are many jobs you can't keep for more than a day—no matter how much you want the experience. It's a question of principle. They can't expect you to stay when they lie to you about the position before you even take it.

I'm in college and the ad says *CASHIER WANTED.*

I apply. Brainless job, I figure, but it stays busy at the gas station, so time will pass quickly.

First day, I get there in my uniform.

The manager, much younger than his lover who owns the place, tells me to work the car-wash controls.

I tell him I applied to be a cashier. I applied to work in the heated booth, with the radio on, taking cash from the customers.

"Mop the bathroom floors, too," he says. "Keep the place clean at all times. We never know when a customer will ask for the key to the restrooms."

It's windy and freezing at the car-wash control box. I don't know why customers bother with a wash on a day like this. It's been raining for days and mud covers their wheels the moment they leave.

But it's a "free" wash. Don't turn anything down if it's free.

Fill your tank. Free car wash.

Free pissing in the bathroom Reed just mopped for you. Reed the fool we just hired. He thought he was going to work the cash register. What we really needed was a mop boy.

Next workday is a Sunday. I have to be at the car-wash control box at seven in the morning, in the freezing rain.

The gas station uniform is neatly folded on the chair next to my bed.

I go back to sleep.

The phone rings at eight.

"You're supposed to be at work," says the boy manager. "You were hired to be dependable, and the company is counting on you."

I was hired to run the cash register. There seems to be another cashier there now. I'll show up when she quits or is murdered.

The boy manager goes into his management philosophy, straight out of a college textbook. Professional Quality Management, he calls it. Every employee in the corporation must start at the bottom, know the business inside and out, be familiar with every position. To reach that optimum of corporate performance, he likes to rotate every new employee through the car-wash station, bathroom maintenance, the cash-register booth, and so forth. Every employee must be trained as if he were on his way to becoming the manager, prepared to do *everything*.

Does that include having sex with the owner?

The boy manager doesn't answer.

Don't bother with my paycheck, I say. I'll keep the uniform as a memento, and we can call it even.

The uniform is still somewhere in my closet. Gas station shirts are much more comfortable than Brooks Brothers corporate straight jackets. It's my first weekiversary at CUD. I would like to stay till the end of the month to get at least one paycheck—to pay for the reverse-pleated trousers and three-button jackets—but the hours are killing me.

Grueling boredom, too.

Senior Project Manager. And they still haven't found a project for me.

It's a growing company, my boss says. Huge staff hired en masse. Complete, daily chaos. I imagine the evacuation of a sinking ship whose captain is utterly drunk and no one knows where he hid the life jackets. That's one more story to tell Dr. Hurt.

The corporate family that gets hired en masse gets laid off en masse. It's bound to happen, soon enough, when CUD's overvalued stock becomes toilet paper.

One paycheck is all I need.

Courage, Mr. Preston. You can make it.

In my short career as a day trader, I have an excellent record. The portfolio's worth a great deal more than the forty thousand I put in it, despite the market's doom-and-gloom decline lamented by analysts. Hewitt's approach really works. I keep on buying and selling—and celebrating with Siesta.

Winnie the Pooh pillowcase for her.

Fruit of the Loom briefs for me.

Faux Chanel No. 5 for her, in spray.

Cuban-seed cigars for me. Not as good as Hewitt's, but close enough.

The next postcard comes from a few blocks away. "Lunch at *Paddy's Buttermilk* pub," it says, followed by a string of numbers making no sense.

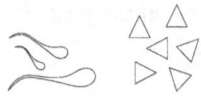

The numbers stand for Paddy's street address, plus the date and time of our meeting.

"Smart boy," Hewitt says when I join him at the booth. "You figured it out. Just the type of mind I want working for me."

I already have a job, Byron. CUD Systems. Can you pay as much?

Hewitt ignores my thoughts as effectively as Gem ever did. I'm sure that's why she never returned to Le Clochard. She figured out my fantasies while sitting right there, just a few tables away. They made her uncomfortable.

Two mugs of Paddy's buttermilk arrive. "This surely is America," Hewitt says. "In Dublin, these would be served in a glass."

"And warm."

"Right you are, Reed. Have I told you I think you have a great genius? That's the honest truth, and I'm not easily impressed by human beings."

Hewitt goes on to describe the many delicious things he had to eat in Europe. Stuffed tortoise in Paris. Turkish olives in Munich. Yellowman in Belfast. His taste for international cuisine comes down from his ancestors, he says. Ancestors are the key to everything.

"Do you know *your* ancestors, Reed?"

"Just mother and father. Haven't seen them since I was fifteen."

Hewitt takes out one of his business cards and puts it upside down on the table. Handwritten on it is *Zachariah Joyce*.

"This is your first assignment. Zach was born in 1812, somewhere in Maryland. A Quaker, I think. He's the starting point of your research. Work back from him. Stick to the past. We'll worry about the more recent generations later. That's when the research becomes interesting."

Hewitt puts the card in my breast pocket. The salary won't be much at first, he says, while I'm on probation. But once I've proven myself, I'll get a raise.

"Do you want the job, Reed?"

Zachariah Joyce. Born 1812. Reed the private investigator, the mediocre cigar smoker, digging up dirt on one Zach Joyce, exposing Zach's nineteenth century indiscretions.

"Remember that young woman at Le Clochard?" I say. "She was always writing. Long hair."

Hewitt cracks a smile. "I met many girls there."

Whore-to-whore salesman.

Door-to-door pimp.

"She had a test tube on her table," I say.

"Oh, Gem! Good old Gem. Yes, of course. Brilliant girl. She's part of our team."

Zach Joyce Investigator: Another trade for my collection.

I'm in.

Part-time genealogist. Researcher. Hewitt team member.

Gem hopeful.

I'm in.

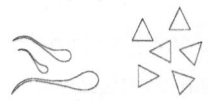

Meetings are what you do at CUD. We spend all our time going to meetings, listening to our strategist boss say things like "torture our competitors" and "skewer their beta versions" between gulps of mineral water from small plastic bottles.

Two dozen of the bottles go on the conference table at the start of every meeting. The boss drinks twenty of them. Pitches the empty ones in a large cardboard box in the corner.

No one's doing any work anywhere. It's all meetings. The strategy changes daily. Whatever the techies are blogging about the market, that's where we're going.

I say nothing. Even if you are a supposed expert—top of the line—people expect you to learn something about your new $210,000-a-year job before you open your mouth at a meeting.

The guy next to me is wearing a $2,000 wool suit with gaudy earrings for cufflinks and a hairpiece. He's the one with a huge photo of his wife on his desk. Hardly any room left for a computer. Married two weeks.

Out in the hallway, I hear our strategist boss tell the newlywed not to be too sure about his marriage, because he'll most probably be having affairs in less than two years. The size of your wife's photo you display, he says, is directly proportional to the size of your soon-to-come infidelity.

The newlywed is furious. "That's *not* true," he whisperyells. I *love* my wife!" Incredible anger in his words. Makes you think he'll be bringing in a large poster of the woman tomorrow.

My salary is directly proportional to my boss' ability as a manure salesman. He's a practitioner of the new economic paradigm—where corporations are not corporations but offices with chairs and conference tables. In charge of it all: The CBO. Chief Bullshitter Officer—a highly skilled salesman selling technology no one understands but everyone expects will make them overnight millionaires. Through accounting scandals and stock-market near collapses, everything remains the same. All it takes is a skilled CBO, no matter what the economy is doing.

Our CBO is the greatest salesman in the world, and a full-time golfer. When he's not wasting our time with strategy meetings, he's out on the green trawling for suckers, also known as investors.

Dilute the stock every eight weeks.

Issue more and more shares.

It's an endless stream of cash from investors that's paying my salary. As long as the investment capital keeps on coming, the fever survives. CUD Systems is a hot company no one can afford not to invest in. The stock's going through the roof, and even I'm buying. Our boss is a genius. In a matter of days, we're all paper millionaires.

I get greedy. My portfolio turns into a CUD Systems powerhouse. The notes I take at meetings have nothing to do with what's being said. I'm writing predictions. The yellow pad is full of numbers. My co-workers think it's my Senior Project Manager budget, but it's my brokerage account's balance, multiplied by the fantasy math of the market.

Our Senior *Senior* Project Manager *Manager*—the Mother of all managers—is talking nonsense at the end of the table. I pretend to take more notes. Switch from numbers to words. "Market share." "Retrofitted software network array." "Archetypal server application."

Should I simply disappear after I cash my first paycheck, or do I get up at one of these meetings and announce my sudden departure? Tell them: "This is one of the most talented teams I've ever had the pleasure of working with. I've been taking notes, going over comments contributed by every member of this highly intelligent group, thinking…What a load of crap."

Or I could simply fake a nervous breakdown and let them slip me a pink slip in the hospital.

Siesta, the voice of reason, tells me to do nothing. Try to keep both jobs for a while. No experience lasts forever, anyway. Everything simply *lasts*. Pushing buttons at a car-wash station. Delivering newspapers. Reaming toilets. Senior-project managing. All turn into one.

Every human's resume should simply say *WORK*, in huge letters, covering the whole page.

Job Experience: *WORK*.

Take it or leave it.

Hewitt says he hires writers because they can relate to his project's goal. We are supposed to trace back all the American Joyce lines to the Irish Joyce lines, and establish who in America is the closest relative to James Joyce. "I want the American Finnegans in my hand," he says—and leaves it at that.

Whatever.

I'm in it for Gem.

And glad when Hewitt finally arranges a meeting.

She picks me up in a cab, dressed completely in red.

Bubbly crazy. Probably on drugs. She laughs and says she's a she-Devil.

I play along—confused. She was always so quiet at the café, writing so seriously. That was the Gem I wanted to meet, the one I thought unattainable. But the precious gemstone turns out to be no gem at all, just stone.

I don't trust experiences where desire easily gets what it wants: before the evening is over, both of us physically entangled.

Too easy. Too soon.

But Gem seems more than ready, as if Hewitt had given her orders. *Spend the night with Reed. It will give him a push to do better genealogical research.*

A pimp, after all.

Whatever he wants.

Red beret. Red kerchief around her neck. Red panties.

I ask her where she was born. How. When.

Learn more about Gem.

She answers with giggles.

I can't get an intelligent word out of her.

Our cab drives past a big neon sign that says *Diskoh*. I look Gem in the eye. "You don't have to speak if you don't want to. Answer with nods."

She nods, and the cab turns left.

"Is this some sort of mission Hewitt put you up to?"

She nods. A sign flashes outside—*Mission Furniture*—and the cab makes another left turn.

"Your parents are dead."

Nod.

"You were an only child and have no close relatives left."

Nod.

There's a funeral home at the corner, and the cab turns left.

"You don't like the color red."

Shake.

Diskoh flies past us again, in bright neon red.

Gem's eyes begin to droop. She has already had her night out. Waiting for her second wind.

I want to ask her whether she's urine or water, but don't dare yet.

Diskoh a third time, then a fourth.

"I was told to drive in circles," the cabbie says.

Drop us off, then, when the neon light comes again.

Don't judge a person by the way she nods. When Gem gets her second wind, we end up inside the Diskoh, where the music is loud and no one examines the present.

I'm not a dancer, Gem. Tried it once. Age fourteen. Classes and all. Parents paid for it. *Dancing lawyers have an edge in the world.*

Didn't do any good.

Gem doesn't care. She drags me to the dance floor.

I can feel the music's throbbing drums disturb the flow in my veins. The moving lights on the ceiling make me think of a bad highway accident. Fire trucks. Ambulances. Gem's red outfit is blood left on the pavement. She puts her lips to my ear and says, "Soon they'll come up with a drug that will make sex obsolete."

Not a chance. At the beginning of every session, Dr. Hurt always asks me what I've wished for in life. "All my life," I tell him, "I've wished I'd been born a woman, but only so I could become a lesbian. What does that mean, Dr. Hurt?"

"I think it means you are happy with your own sexuality, but don't quote me on that."

In one form or another, sex is always on our minds. How can it become obsolete?

The music reaches a peak, then the mix comes in. All a confusion of drums and guitars for a few seconds, followed by a new song—a sun emerging from a storm.

A woman dancing alone next to us is in a trance.

We change our dance routine to accommodate the new beat.

"Feeling horny?" Gem asks. "Fill a prescription!"

"I have an idea for a story about a world crisis in the Catholic Church," I tell Dr. Hurt.

He's so interested, his pen runs out of ink and I have to wait while he performs a refill.

"Why don't you use a Bic, like everyone else?"

"Plastic pens, Reed? No way. Leave the future to the fools who'll suffer through it. Your Catholic yarn...does it take place in Ireland?"

No. The setting is Rome. And the plot is very simple: Italian revolution, followed by dictatorship, bombs, mayhem and Papal eviction. Then the fascists turn the Vatican into a theme park.

"Pharmasex," Gem whispers in my ear.

I get the message.

After two discos and a loud nightclub, we end up in a motel room.

She's all over me. "You're Gem's doctor," she says. "Fill my prescription."

The heat in her words reminds me of *The Combustioneer*, another long-ago idea I shared with Dr. Hurt.

In life, everything burns, especially bridges. That was the novel's opening sentence. After a few successful acts of pyromania, the main character, nicknamed "the Flame Fiend" by the police, embarks on nightly outings of arson and poetic extravaganza. The

Fiend leaves a poem inside a fireproof cartouche at the scene of every one of his crimes.

> *O water can't touch us!*
> *From the hydro canons of hate,*
> *My love, I'll protect you.*
> *I'm enthralled by your beauty,*
> *As free as an ember,*
> *My fire, my love, my flame.*

Or something like that. The point was not the quality of his poems but the professionalism and detail with which he planned and executed his nightly conflagrations. The media made a sensation out of every little flame, never allowing the public to forget that the Fiend was out there. The police and fire departments held daily news conferences to subtly urge and taunt the Fiend to act again. Otherwise, how would they ever catch him?

That was the moral dilemma: No one wanted another business or factory to go up in flames, but everyone wanted the Flame Fiend to act again, and again. If he stopped now, he would never get caught. And that wouldn't satisfy the public's sense of justice. In any criminal case, it's better to have more victims than no one to punish for the crime.

Among my own ashes, Gem's gone before I open my eyes in the morning.

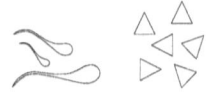

When you lose your shirt on an investment, remember you never had a shirt to begin with. Wardrobes are illusions.

CUD's stock has gone sour. Big deal. Revenge of the market on insider traders. Technically, I'm not an insider since I've practically quit CUD. But my portfolio is now worth twenty grand and I owe my credit cards over forty.

Twenty grand in the hole.

Overnight.

Day trader during the day. Bankrupt loser pharmacist during the night. Everything burns, especially bridges.

Hewitt suggests a meeting, but I don't want to talk to him.

Let the phone ring.

Go out for a walk.

Don't bother with CUD. Quit by no-show.

The first direct-deposit paycheck is already in the bank. It should be enough.

Sell all the stock.

Pay off the credit cards.

Buy Siesta nothing.

Start from scratch.

The Abandoner. The story of a successful, intelligent writer who hits it big with a string of three insanely lucrative books. Then, he completely abandons writing, and surprises everyone by taking up biology and becoming a hugely successful scientist, then a musician—with three Platinum records—then a politician, then a badminton pro and the reason for a sudden surge in the popularity of the sport. Then an industrialist, inventor, and movie mogul. Everything he does, he turns into success right before he abandons it. *The Abandoner.* I think I shared the story with Dr. Hurt at some point.

Books coming out of my ears.

Stories that never get written.

That's what makes it so depressing to go in a bookstore. Shelf after shelf of evidence that others can finish what they begin. Stacks of new volumes on several tables. *New Releases.* New evidence.

A large banner above says, "A new book by local author Wallace Hur." *The Pope's Exile.* "Meet the author tonight." They have a photocopy of the book's back cover taped to the window. "When a new dictator takes control of Italy," it says, "he evicts the Pope from the Vatican and turns Saint Peter's Basilica into a theme park."

Wallace Hur.

That son-of-a-pen Dr. Hurt, making it as a writer with his discipline and my ideas.

Wallace Hur. He thinks he can disguise his theft by using a pen name, dropping a tee.

Dr. Hurt hurts me, with one book after another.

The Backyard Explorer.

God is Electric.

The Combustioneer.

All of my titles. Maybe that's how successful writers really do it. They are all doctors or priests or in some other position of confidence that involves other human beings telling them all their stories—stories they turn into books. Stephen King's real name: Dr. Frank Kingdell. Sue Grafton: Sister Susana of the Order of Christ. Tom Wolfe: Counselor Thomas Fox.

Wallace Hur's latest book opens with a short sentence: "The Pope was sad."

I can't stand it, and walk away—unable to stop thinking about it.

It makes the reader wonder what the Pope might call sad.

I don't want to know.

Look at the cars.

Look at the crowds, Christmas-shopping in July.

Everyone's buying other people's books.

I take refuge in my favorite park, where the squirrels are having a feast and not writing.

Squirrels can be fried. You start by cutting the skin around their paws and pulling it off the flesh as if peeling a banana.

For Immediate Release: New Duce Shuts Down Vatican. Saint Peter's to Become Next Disneyland.

Blasphemy.

Make sure to remove the scent glands on the inside of the squirrel's forelegs. If you forget to do so, the meat will taste like it was cooked in urine.

My first Senior Project Manager paycheck comes up short in covering my Day Trader's portfolio losses, so I go to work for Hewitt.

The first step is to yawn away an afternoon at Le Clochard, reading how-to genealogy books. You can't be a genealogist if you are not a *certified* genealogist, the book says. Practitioners must pass a test. They must join a professional organization, flash their certificates at every turn.

The point is to keep people out—to exclude, to monopolize knowledge and keep everyone who is not a member of the organization in the dark.

Knowledge-prevention institutions are very active these days. Most research libraries qualify. *Open only to certified, professional researchers,* their signs say.

Don't worry about it, Hewitt tells me. He knows the right people. Signs me up for a seminar. Six hours of boredom. Diploma in hand. Done: you're a professional genealogist.

Everyone talks at the same time at the seminar. Me, me, me. My ancestors are more important than yours, says one. I have Irish, Belgian, Chinese and Peruvian blood in me, says another.

It's important to them—to have all these connections to the past.

I have jack of all trades. I have Siesta. I have time.

And I wouldn't be in this bloodline-boasting session if it weren't for Hewitt.

I wonder if Gem went through it, as well. *She's not what you think*, I keep telling myself. Gem the Disco Queen, the wet nurse dressed in bright cherry.

I need a second opinion.

A second date.

Maybe a blind date—eyes truly shut.

It's something marriage counselors haven't tried yet. Tell couples in trouble: *Go home, put on blindfolds, and live like that for a full week before reporting back to me. Create a need. You can't hate those you can't see.*

The ancestral-pining session goes into full-boredom mode.

We break for lunch. But before they let us eat, someone yells at the group that now is the time to sign up for a Heritage Tour. "Don't just talk about your ancestors. Go visit their graves!" a woman yells.

She's pushy—approaches everyone with a full-color brochure covered with photos of grandmas. "No need to see your travel agent," she says. "Just give me your credit card number and I'll guide you back to your roots."

Heritage Tour Packages. Book now before you join them in death.

Chelton, the man with Irish-Chinese-Peruvian-plus blood offers me a sandwich.

"How did you get interested in your ancestry?" he asks.

My answer doesn't really matter. He wants to tell me how *he* got into it. "Fell in love with my grandmother," he says. "She was long dead when I first set eyes on a photograph of her. She's gorgeous."

Don't tell me more, Chelton. I don't want to know.

But he insists. Shows me a photo of the love of his life.

"They don't make women like this anymore."

They sure don't, Chelton, not with those feathery hats and rib-busting corsets. Looks more like a great-great-grandma to me.

Maybe Chelton is one of those trailing offspring—born when his father was in his sixties—with paternal grandparents already long gone, two or three generations ago.

"Look at her eyes," he says. "Isn't she pretty?"

I can see why he likes her. He has her eyes. Carbon copies. The woman in the photograph could be his twin sister.

How many men—if they could go back in time—would marry their own mothers or grandmothers, meeting them by chance, not knowing who they were?

How many bosses are consciously afraid of their secretaries?

My CUD secretary, Mrs. Rushmore, calls me at home.

"Mr. Preston? Is that you?"

No, ma'am. You have the wrong number—and do you know you woke me up twice already, and I just came in from my night shift at the paper mill and really need to get some sleep?

"I apologize, sir. You sound so much like Mr. Preston. Sorry."

Poor thing. I shouldn't do that to Mrs. Rushmore. She's a nice, plump, middle-aged grandmother. Four grandchildren. Not yet married to any of them.

I should disconnect the phone. Spare her.

But not Gem.

I need an explanation from Gem.

When I ask her to meet me, the first thing she says is she's bipolar. Her moods swing from utterly calm to totally wild and exuberant. She tells me to disregard the red dress and the medical talk of our Diskoh night. It wasn't the real her, just behavior that resurfaces—maybe—once a year? She's not sure herself. Doesn't even remember what we did that night. Hopes she didn't hurt me.

If it doesn't hurt, it's not working, Dr. Hurt likes to say.

Hurt me more, Gem. It's alright.

But she's not a Disco Queen. Disco is the "up" side of her personality. The high. The giddy, bubbly end of her bipolar pole. She tries to control the extremes in her behavior with medication, but that backfires sometimes.

Pharmasex.

The real Gem is the down-in-the-dumps Gem, she says. When she's down, she writes. She does research. She truly enjoys life. It's a good thing she's down most of the time.

That sounds extreme, Gem. Wouldn't it be better to have a little of the Disco Queen around for the weekend? For balance?

No. She's perfectly happy with her life.

From red-nurse lover to grandmother...
In a fraction of my lifetime.

The Flame Fiend strikes again.
The Love Fiend.

Pharmacalm in the morning.
Pharmadecorum in the evening.
Pharmacelibate all night.

It's not what I wanted, either, so I go home for a consolation prize: Siesta.

If it doesn't hurt, it's not working.

Gem. Siesta. I'll have to buy a new pillow.

And the phone rings.

And I don't answer.

Still haven't disconnected the service.

They don't make pillows like they used to, either. Split seams.

Ring. Ring. "Pay attention to me."

Humans and pillows. The stock has suffered.

Ring.

The last night of Disco.

Tease me, then take it away.

No use in dreaming of Gem as a girlfriend if there's no future with her.

"Let's be friends," she said. "We'll be working with Byron A. Hewitt."

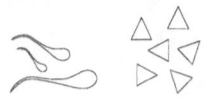

After a few beers at Paddy's Buttermilk, I'm slightly drunk as I enter the movie theater. It's late, but the place is packed. I don't know if it's Tuesday or Friday. The week gets lost in the calendar when genealogical research takes hold of your life.

I bought a new Siesta today and still have it with me in its plastic store bag. The drunks at Paddy's looked at me funny when they noticed it.

Why's that guy drinking beer with a pillow under his ass?

I'm glad they couldn't see the commemorative Lady Di pillowcase folded inside. Paid fourteen bucks for it. Strong seams. Nice design.

The audience sits obediently as the lights go down. We're ready to partake in the entertainment we're about to receive. Thank you, God, for fantasy, for letting the cab drivers in the audience dream that they are private investigators who only drive a cab as a cover.

We all like to believe we're ordinary people living extraordinary lives. Writers are notorious for it. There's no reason to write fiction other than as therapy for the writer who's thoroughly unhappy with reality. A banker who loves his job doesn't become a fiction writer. A banker who loves his job doesn't become anything other than a banker.

The rest of us escape our professions with the help of whatever tools are at hand. Music. Movies. Books. Wishes and dreams. We become jacks of all escapes.

With urinal reaming and senior-project managing, I've had all the escape I need lately. I relax as the movie begins. Siesta gives me comfort. In the dark, I rip off the plastic—quickly, to keep it from crunching—and slip the new pillowcase on her.

Comfort as a substitute for popcorn.

I set my wristwatch alarm to wake me up in twenty-five minutes, when the movie's first plot point arrives. Any American movie with hopes of success requires two plot points and a murder. You can time all Hollywood productions aimed at a mass audience. Minute 25 represents the twenty-fifth page of the script. A plot point on page 25 is *mandatory*. An event that sends the story line in a completely different direction, just about the time when the audience is beginning to get bored with the old line.

There's nothing new about this movie. It's been done before. But the special effects are supposed to be better. John Lester, a brilliant scientist, is shrunk to the size of a human cell, and sent on his way, with a microscopic video camera, to explore the inner workings of the human body.

He's deposited on a slice of cold pizza, and when his wife takes a bite, we're inside his camera on the way to her stomach. From there, it's off to the intestines and, through the capillaries, into her bloodstream and the wonders of cellular activity.

Hollywood the teacher, educating the public on human biology.

Life and reality as a series of plot points.

Three billion pairs of chemical bases in John Lester's wife's body. Impossible to cover them all in a two-hour movie. A scientist-inside-a-dog movie would be more manageable. Dogs are one of the most genetically engineered products on earth. Artificially bred by humans through domestication for at least a hundred thousand years. The dog genome is a cinch, Hewitt says. He explained it to me at his favorite Chinese restaurant.

Hewitt knows more about genetics than all the scientists at the National Institutes of Health combined, he says. The recipient of a "genius" grant, modesty apart. He set out to work with the dog genome, but gave up. "Too simple. Let the lesser minds map it and sequence it."

I may be through pitching TV shows to producers, but movie ideas keep on coming to mind. This one's about a child who wants to establish paternity among several potential fathers. The boy's mother has suffered a nervous breakdown from which she will never recover. She has taken permanent residence in some sort of institution where thinking is not allowed.

The boy has a box full of love letters to go by. He's a teenager, and all the letters are dated one or two years prior to his conception. Passionate letters. His mother liked to jump from one lover to another, and back. She must have known that all those love affairs would someday drive her out of her mind, so she had kept the love letters to help in her treatment.

The boy takes the box to the mental institution. Doctor sees them, reads them, disapproves of them, and sends them back home with the boy.

Then comes the emotional music. The boy reads the letters, and his voice turns into his mother's voice as he reads. An *emotional voiceover*, as they say in the industry. He is ONE with his MOM. Tears running down his cheeks. *Academy Award.*

Plot point.

Determination.

Sweet boy turns into purpose-filled maniac. He's going to find out who his father is if it's the last thing he does.

Goes to every one of the potential twenty-three candidates.

None wants to cooperate. Not interested in children.

He stalks them all. Breaks into their homes. Steals fingernail clippings and other human waste from their bathrooms that allows him to collect DNA samples on the suspects and compare them to his own DNA.

Case solved.

Time to file the lawsuit.

Page 120 of the script: Boy has proven his love for his mother.

A great little movie with great first-weekend grosses. A hit at the box office. Based on the best-selling novel by Reed Lodge, successful author.

Books should be more like scripts, Siesta says.

Two-hour books.

120 Pages.

"A page that takes more than a minute to read has too much text on it. Cut it until the ink is in balance." *How to Write a Bestseller*. Chapter One: "If you give them a page a minute, they'll recommend the book, even if they don't like it."

The one-sitting novel.

Entertainment that doesn't tax the mind.

Locust of the Mind doesn't fit the mold, I realize. It's for a niche market. But it's not too late to revise it. Turn it into a movie-novel. Two plot points and a murder. Hundreds of characters, all appearing for just one second, where the main character—my alter ego— endures through a sea of peripheral nobodies.

Someone says, "Shhh!" when my wristwatch goes off.

We're in the midst of fill-in movie dialog. Not meant to be communicative. Just another sound effect.

The scientist's nickname appears to be Johnny. We hear his wife call him so every five seconds. He is in constant communication with her through wireless headphones. You'd think the electronic equipment would get dirty with all the lipids, cell soups, and plasma he's swimming in. But never mind.

"Johnny!"

Waves of red liquid splash all around him.

"What are you doing, Johnny?"

"Just a second, hon." Johnny's busy pulling strings of nerves, or something, out of his way as he advances through the brambles and jungles of endoplasmic mystery.

"Johnny, stop that. Those are my ovaries. Get out!"

The audience laughs. A little comic relief before the scheduled plot point.

"Johnny, stop. No...Johnny..."

The plot point is not an ovarian orgasm but the sudden arrival of a second scientist—a mad scientist, by the way the make-up artists have twisted his hair—who approaches the writhing wife as she stands next to the lab counter, and puts her out with a rag soaked in chloroform.

CUT TO: The woman's cellular insides. Johnny has definitely been affected by the anesthetic. He's bumping and tossing around, as if inside a sinking submarine in a 1940s Hollywood studio.

"Johnny, we're lost..."

The last bit of dialog to reach me.

Drift back to sleep.

I forget to set the watch for the second plot point.

When I wake, the credits are rolling.

The auditorium is nearly empty, but the names roll endlessly on.

Cast. Grips. Assistants and gaffers. Caterers. Assistants to the assistants. Hair stylists. Best boy. Foley artists.

A never-ending list of perpetrators.

Alan Baker.

Christopher Frank.

Tess Bennett.

Marian Lawrence.

I can imagine each one of them attending a genealogy seminar.

The instructor says, "Ladies and gentlemen, begin mapping your family trees...NOW!"

And they go. Family tree: Root. Trunk. Branch. Leaf.

Flower, fruit and seed.

And they find out, after a few retro-generations, that they're all related. Cast. Crew. Producers. Caterers. All meant to come together to make this film, because it was in their genes.

Johnny's Biological Pizza Journey—the movie.

It just had to be made.

"All humans are subject to the Law of Increasing Demand," Hewitt says. One of his favorite subjects at our weekly Chinese feast. "Children begin their demands early. Toys. Christmas gifts. Birthday presents. Up to about age thirteen. Then the needs switch to clothes and music...."

As we go through life, he says, the demands increase tenfold. Once finished with high school, the grown children need a college degree, plus the drugs and free sex that come with the campus lifestyle.

Then the search for a suitable mate.

Marriage.

Cars.

House.

Children.

Nothing is ever enough.

The next demand is to become independently wealthy—a savvy, admired industrialist.

Followed by me, me, me media attention, before turning into an accomplished air balloonist traversing the earth from the South Pole to the North. Daring part-time explorer in thick wool sweaters and a goatee.

And don't forget the pipe—for the look.

"Image is everything," Hewitt says. "Get a tan from the polar ice, and start a new trend. That's the next wish on the list of life: become a trendsetter. Have stuff named after you."

The Byron A. Hewitt Polar Tan.

Byron Polar Tours. $40,000 weekend getaways, with Byron-brand parka and sunglasses included. Leave the office on Friday. Show up on Monday with your authentic polar tan. Tell your co-workers how you roasted a polar bear for lunch and drank polar-ice whiskey sours.

Make them jealous.

Create envy.

They'll want polar bear, too.

That's the Law of Increasing Demand: When we have it all but still *must* have that Polar Experience, or life won't be complete.

When our fortune cookies come, Hewitt ignores his. Doesn't need reassurances. Doesn't need hope.

Mine says, *He who knows he has enough is rich.*

Beautifully said beautiful bullshit.

No one ever knows.

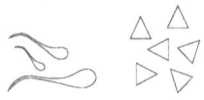

To be able to endure it, genealogical research must be mixed with live entertainment. Hewitt said to concentrate on Zachariah Joyce and his ancestors. But that can wait. I am more interested in Zach manifestations in the flesh, as found in one of his descendents at a gym called *Hard*.

They don't call these places gyms anymore because that sounds too athletic. I'm at the Hard Health Club, advertised in the paper with a promise: *We'll get you hard, or your money back.*

I don't undress because I don't want stares.

Genealogists turn pale and flabby in a matter of days. All that research-library fluorescent lighting and sugary snacks.

Everyone else on the Club's floor is a life-sized action figure, in tight underwear and shiny, shaved bare chests.

No women.

The Hard caters only to men, a special sort of them.

I've seen these men's ads in the classifieds. *Toned, exceedingly intelligent Breeder. Available for in-vitro, flesh-to-flesh, or surrogate conception. Reasonable fees. Call Roger at...*

I traced this Breeder down from one of Zach's many sons. He goes by the name Ian Reeves, though he is still part of the Joyce male line. Genes don't care about surnames.

Ian's newspaper ad emphasizes reasonable fees.

Monthly membership at the Hard is $650.

Half the men working out here have forty-million-dollar infertility insurance. Breeder coverage, as the industry calls it.

When the men are not working the sperm-bank circuit, this is where they improve themselves. Brains are important to sperm buyers, but so are muscles, and these specimens have plenty of them.

If I were a customer, I wouldn't pay much for Ian. His cells seem to have forgotten the growth-spurt sessions of his teen years. His muscles may be hard, but they don't stretch out anywhere. A ball of human fitness. It looks like he picked the wrong profession. In a better life, he'd be a jack of all trades. A construction worker. A wrestler. Professional diver. Third-grade football coach.

"Ian Reeves?" I ask.

He may have been reading my mind. Not a very welcoming man. Hard at work at getting hard.

Bench-pressing fifty, eighty, three-hundred pounds.

I'll wait, I say.

He doesn't react.

Huff. Huff. Huff.

Loins of steel.

I wonder if Zach was this athletic. His last will and testament says he was a "Planter." That's what they used to call farmers in colonial days. Planters were fit men. No air-conditioned tractors with CD players and snack bars available to them.

A horse, maybe.

Huff. Huff.

If he could afford one.

Zach was probably a tobacco planter. Free to smoke his crop and sell it without fear of lung-cancer lawsuits.

Huff. Huff. Huff.

What you give your clients is in your germ cells, Ian. No amount of exercise can change what's in them.

Most of his clients don't know that.

Huff. Huff. Huff.

Ian takes his time.

Makes me think of a bored prostitute.

Slow client.

Huff. Huff. Huff.

Finish up, already! Got other Johns waiting.

An American prostitute sleeps with an average 648 men each year. Zillions of germ cells wasted.

Huff. Huff.

One million women ply the trade in America.

Huff. Hu…

Ian's finished.

He smiles. Not reading my mind, after all. Just being professional about his workout.

He's starving, he says, and proposes lunch.

We sit by the Club's outdoor pool, in a forest of white, steel-and-glass tables shaded by canvass.

Palm trees all around.

This is Florida. Research trip paid for by Hewitt.

Reed—the broke, former Senior Project Manager—deserves to start his new job with a sunny vacation.

I had to tell Hewitt that some of Zach's records had ended up in a Florida Historical Society archive.

Not a full lie. Ian's a living record of Zach's male chromosome. The Y chromosome. It passes from man to son, generation after generation, virtually unchanged. Only rare mutations interfere.

I order a sandwich.

Ian says he brown-bags his lunch, although the bag is not brown but white canvass.

Inside: baby-food jars.

"Do you know how many of these you can get for a hundred bucks?" he asks. "Sixty-nine cents apiece when on sale. Gerber's *Tender Harvest*. Organically Grown. Zero fat. Two hundred milligrams of potassium, which 'may lower the risk of stroke,' 'may be effective in treating rheumatoid arthritis,' and may do a long list of other chemical tricks. As long as the claims are preceded by the word *may*, everything's fine with the world. No one has lied. No manufacturer is a mountebank."

Ian's not a food crank, he says. For some reason, he just loves baby food. Can't get enough of it.

I ask if he's married.

No. Breeders are delicate things, he says. Marriage *may* dilute sperm counts.

Ian has never heard of Zachariah Joyce. And he's not interested, even when I tell him he could increase his fees by using his pedigree in his ads. It always impresses sperm clients when the donor has taken the time to check his genetic background.

My research doesn't prove anything, Ian says. Just a bunch of court records and documents that should have burned in some colonial fire or been eaten by moths.

"Only one thing is certain," he says. "I'm here as the result of a whole lotta fucking." And he bursts into uncontrollable baby-food laughter.

Breeder humor.

Not that delicate, after all. The words "fucking" and "organic baby food" don't seem to go on the same supermarket isle.

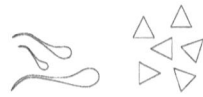

When you're a Senior Project Manager, even if you do zilch all day, the nine-to-seven schedule grinds your brain.

Just being there.

The electromagnetic waves from coffee machines, microwave ovens, computers and copiers must have something to do with it.

One-track thinking environments.

A learning victim's hell.

By contrast, research is heaven.

The beach is my library. I'm an honorary genealogist grubbing imaginary roots in the sands of Florida.

The Joyce roots.

I wish Hewitt had chosen Flagler as the target last name. A paperback someone left in my motel room says that Henry Morrison Flagler made Florida. He started making money at age fourteen in Ohio. Five dollars a month in 1844. He went from dealing with grain to peddling salt, and back to grain again.

Then he met Rockefeller.

Went into oil. Hotels. Railways. Florida.

On the plane back to the cold, I think of what it might be like to own a hotel with more than a thousand rooms, like Flagler. The wealthy know how to complicate their lives, just like desperate writers know how to complicate their language.

I try to add a few meaningless pages to *Locust of the Mind*, but it's hard to write on a plane. The woman next to me keeps on trying to look at my text.

I *think* it's a woman.

Sometimes you can't tell.

I write the word "androgynous" and move the pad just enough so sHe can read it.

Chapter title: *The Inherent Genetic Superiority of Androgynous Beings.*

After two paragraphs of scientific praise, I switch tack:

Whatever the benefits, this utterly flawed genetic makeup cannot but engender monstrous mutations that may threaten the entire fabric of society, not to mention democracy, liberty, and professional sports.

No reaction from seat 12B. I continue:

Parents who find out their embryos are infected with the androgynous knots of twisted DNA—the so-called p43 protein reacting with the dl21 mitochondrial aberration—are best advised to try again, after flushing the invader from their children's inheritance.

I order a whiskey.

Close my eyes and try to look scientific.

Passengers shouldn't stick their noses into other people's literary armpits. If there were a law that forced authors to make their first drafts available before completing their manuscripts, no books would ever get written. First drafts are like picking your nose. You don't do it in public.

Our captain recites a canned message about bad weather, and the plane soon goes into roller-coaster mode. *Folks, prepare for a rough landing.*

sHe's holding tight to 12B.

When the flight attendant collects my glass, I rip the androgynous chapter off the pad, crumple it, and give it to her. "Could you please toss this in the trash?"

The flight attendant rushes off. The plane rolls and coasts. A sudden void in our stomachs.

"They don't serve booze when you most need it," I tell 12B. sHe's fixed on the ball of paper as it's taken away to a landfill.

With only a small backpack for luggage, I take a bus and walk home from the airport. It's late—and cold.

There's a recording studio five blocks from the house. A couple of musicians are taking a break outside, talking riffs and chords and what have you. It's better to hear what their music sounds like in notes than in words, so I wait for them to finish their break. Walk in. Greet everyone as if I were paying their rent, their utility and grocery bills. When a shady producer is your only source of income, he owns you.

I know the studio's owner.

Used to ream his toilets.

He's not in, so I have more freedom to pretend. Serve myself a drink. Talk shop with the boys.

A recording engineer comes out of a booth. Says, "Hi, Bob."

That's all right. You can call me Bob.

The nice thing about rock-star wannabes and their retinues is that they're doing what they really love. There are no sour faces in the recording studio. This is their dream.

The lead singer is laying down his tracks, on his own. He has the best job in the house. Lead-singing: a no-luggage profession. No instruments to carry around. No music to learn. No need to get in- volved with the electronics of the process. Just your voice and per- sonality to accompany you. And the extra credit that comes with being a band's front man, even when you don't write the songs, or the music.

The rest of the band spends countless hours rehearsing, recording and mixing—getting it perfect. Then you come into the recording booth by yourself, hear what the others have previously recorded through a pair of headphones, and sing to it as the engineer adds another track to the project.

I would like to be a lead singer—the height of simplicity in career minimalism.

Just look at him. Probably got up at noon. Had breakfast at two. Spent the day at a bar, talking with friends. Came to work late. And now, there he stands, one hand on his headphones, the other one waving, conducting his voice. A clean-cut boy. New jeans. Doc Martens. White shirt. All music. Destined for money.

I can imagine him going home to an empty apartment, a place where no clutter lives. He's a monk who lives in simplicity. Owns nothing. Keeps it spiritual.

The ideal life.

On the other hand, minimalism is useless if a global disaster ever strikes. Farmers, for example, would be much better prepared for it than a lead singer. They inhabit the opposite end of the lead singer's life. They're loaded with clutter all through their earthly existence—farm equipment, animals, bills. Mortgages. Crops. Pesticides.

But when mayhem arrives, a farmer can set to work, grow food for himself and his family, use the tools that he has, his skills and his land. Survival is at least a possibility for him.

Whoever has something in hand will be given more, and whoever has nothing will be deprived of even the little they have.

The lead singer, stuck in his minimalist life—in his empty apartment—can only starve. He has no clutter. No tools to survive.

I want to be a farmer.

A lead singer *and* a farmer. A recording engineer and a janitor. A Senior Project Manager and a beautician. A cyclist and a test pilot. A billionaire of the mind, loaded with a wealth of experience. With Hewitt, I'm a researcher. With a recording engineer, I'm a rock star. With *Locust of the Mind*, I'm a psychosexual-science writer.

As far as I can remember, there were always shrinks lurking around my early childhood, carefully disguised as school teachers and family friends. Their principal job: to push an illustrated book depicting occupations and professions. Colorful drawings of a happy fireman. A happy policeman. Happy nurse.

Everyone happy.

Yes, Reed. You can only become ONE thing when you grow up. So pay attention and make up your mind NOW.

They make sure that children get it imprinted in their brains at a very early age: *The good life is lived by happy workers doing repetitive work.*

Otherwise, Fantasyland falls apart.

In bed with Siesta, I wake up from a bad dream, one of those when you realize you're in your forties and find out you still haven't graduated from high school. Your old principal, Mr. Abrams, gives you a call to say there was a mistake on your transcript. Turns out you never completed such-and-such course. *Your graduation is hereby void.*

"You can't graduate until you pick your monomind career," Mr. Abrams says. "You do what the school board dictates."

I refuse. Why can't a student become a policeman, a fireman, *and* a nurse—by age thirty—and then go on to something else?

He accuses me of dilettantism—the worst possible insult anyone can spray on a jack of all trades.

Spray away, Abrams! There's a big difference between being a collector of experiences and an *experiencer* of experiences. Once you truly chew something, the flavor stays with you forever.

In the morning, Siesta says I should take the day off.

Been working too hard. Thinking too much.

She proposes a day of OWT—One With Time—a game whose purpose, she says, is to throw my mind into a trance from sheer repetitive action. I'm to open the bedroom door, walk to the kitchen, open the refrigerator door, close it. Back to the bedroom. Close the door, then say, "Count your blessings."

The goal is for me to become so engrossed with repetition that the ensuing trance-like state allows me to see time for what it really is—a human construct.

Time doesn't exist, Siesta says. Like Father's Day, it was created by marketers in order to sell something. The proof is in all the ads selling clocks and watches everywhere. Don't be fooled.

I get into the game, intoxicated by the repetition and monotony of it all. I think of those testing facilities at industrial-design firms, where a quality-management robot opens and closes a refrigerator door thousands of times to see how long the gaskets last, how many days after the warranty expires the hinges can be calibrated to collapse.

Siesta proposes ten hours of One With Time action today.

Ten hours of bedroom, kitchen, bedroom and door. Plus count my blessings. Again and again. Love my blessings. Bedroom. Kitchen. Bedroom. Blessed.

Doubly blessed.

I'm one with time—in a trance. Your whole universe happens at once when you OWT. I can see my father, staring at my mother's crotch as I'm being born. And I can see my parents being born, and it's my second birthday, and Napoleon is invading Russia, with me on a horse next to him, and my high school graduation is in progress. I did finish that course, after all. Night school. Nursery school. College. Everything is happening now—forever. You just don't know it until Siesta tells you how to play One With Time.

Count your blessings.

It turns out my parents are no longer alive. During a break from genealogical research, I look them up in the Social Security Death Index. And there they are.

Look up my name.

Nothing.

I'm still alive.

Enter my high school girlfriend's name.

She's not listed, still alive.

My parents: Dad comes up dead years ago.

Mom? Six months ago.

Maybe.

This is just a library. Just the Internet. The information comes from a screen. Records from a database. How real can they be?

Gem's name? Not a clue.

Don't even know where she is.

Hewitt says he's sent her to Ireland. I don't know what to believe.

Hewitt's name is not listed, either.

Alive. Still.

I switch to the electronic phone books and look up my long-lost cousin Paul. Every phone and address in the U.S. checked in five seconds. Paul's not a hermit. He's listed under three phone numbers. Same address. Still in town. Still my cousin.

Give him a call.

"I heard my mother died a few months ago," I tell him.

Paul's a jerk about it. I can tell he feels he's talking to the blackest sheep of the clan. The rotten apple of the family tree. Reed the runaway, the jack of all trades, the amount-to-nothing parasite.

"I have a stack of boxes in my basement," he says. It's all junk to him but, out of respect for my mother, he hasn't thrown them in the trash.

Thanks, Paul.

"Why don't you come get them? That is, if you care at all."

Extra emphasis on *care*.

Paul is conveniently not home when I get there. His wife opens the door. The most gorgeous fat woman I've seen in my life. Shiny, tight skin. Not the obesity of ripples and rolls, the type the fashion industry puts down like the plague. This is pure beauty.

The main drawback of being fat is not the flab itself but the force of gravity. If human bodies were not affected by it, like helium-filled balloons, the pages of *Vogue* would be covered with three- and four-hundred pounders.

Paul's wife has inflated leather for skin. Everything is pulled up, out, and hard. You feel like hugging her.

"I'm so sorry Paul's not home," she says for the fourth time.

Paul's upstairs, of course. Studying me from somewhere. Staring with his overfed children, whispering to them: *That's cousin Reed. He's one clown short of a circus.*

**

At home, I go through Mom's belongings. Mine now. Cases of documents, old letters, discolored photographs of people nobody knows.

Maybe I was adopted.

There was a great deal of infertility on my father's side. Never mind that he came from a family of twelve. All seven girls grew up to become nuns, either by choice or genetic disposition. The boys married, but only my father had a child. I'm the sole heir. The totem pole of a once leafy family tree.

My parents were also the only ones who didn't divorce. They just died early in order to do themselves part.

Their son, the non-lawyer. Too much grief for them.

I apologize.

If I run into adoption papers in one of these boxes, it will explain everything. But all I see are old letters from "Aunt Martha." Not even Mother met the famous Aunt Martha. The letters came down to us from some soul deep in the past. Martha's curly prose deserves the attention of a professional genealogist, the care of an active historical society.

Ten cardboard boxes full of letters from Aunt Martha. I load them in a cab. The driver curses. "Cabs are not UPS."

I tell him the boxes have historical value.

To him, history is dead. He fled his country of birth, he says, precisely to leave his past behind and build a new future, for himself and his children—driving a cab.

"Twelve years in the U.S.," he says. Children happily in college. On their way. "They're going to be lawyers and doctors—all of them."

The volunteer running the historical society feigns interest in my boxes. "We can look at them," she says. "How many do you have?"

"Just a few."

Every time I unload a new box from the cab and place it on her desk, she sighs: "Oh, no. They're big, aren't they?" She asks for my address to return what they can't use. Probably most of it, she warns me.

I give her Paul's.

At home, there's an overnight envelope leaning against the front door. Plane tickets. Hewitt is sending me to San Francisco.

Instructions: Interview Roberta Joyce, an eighty-seven-year-old gold mine of genealogical information.

Hewitt's most unusual request: If Roberta smokes, I should steal her cigarette butts. If she doesn't, I should ask to use her bathroom and steal her toothbrush.

Additional duties: Take photographs. Record our conversation.

Hope she doesn't mind.

But she does mind. Sitting in her dark living room, she seems very suspicious of the proceedings. "You a real, certified genealogist?" she asks. "Or some kind of government meddler?"

I show her my seminar certificate and ask her to smile.

Flash.

Photo-op for the oldest Joyce on the West Coast. I take several shots before proceeding with the interview.

"Tell me about your family, Mrs. Joyce."

"*Ms.* Joyce, young man. I never married."

I don't see an ashtray anywhere, but I came prepared. Pull out a pack of cigarettes. Mind if I smoke, Ms. Joyce?

She does.

"I was born in 1912," she starts without prompting. "The year of the *Titanic* and Gene Kelly. My great grandmother died a few years later. Don't remember which year, but it was on Christmas Day. A tragic day for me because I had looked forward to Christmas all year, and Santa was pushed aside that day, on account of her death. It's like having a child born on your wedding anniversary—a date filled with fear and loathing, and the double reminder of your life's two major mistakes."

May I use the bathroom, Ms. Joyce?

Down the hall.

The door doesn't lock, and the old hinges keep it ajar unless I hold it tight by the doorknob. The toilet's in dire need of a good reaming. Ms. Joyce doesn't do any cleaning.

I fill her rinsing cup in the sink and pour it slowly in the toilet.

Pretend pee.

"Don't take too long," she says out there. "I may have to use the john myself."

Her toothbrush looks like it's never been rinsed. I wrap it in a wad of toilet paper.

Mission accomplished.

I go out and take additional photos, listen to an endless narration of her early years, and then have some tea.

"How did you know I wasn't dead yet?" she asks.

I tell her about the Death Index. She's never heard of it. Never heard of a lot of things. Doesn't watch television.

"The *IN*-ternet? What is that?"

I turn on the recorder and ask her to go back to her grandparents. Details. Where they were born. Who they were. What they did. If her memory is good and she tells me the truth, at some point I should be able to link her to the Breeder in Florida.

Roberta does better than knowing about her grandfather. She brings out a portrait of her great grandfather sitting with a child. "1849," she says. "My grandfather with his dad."

I take notes, a photo of the photograph, and let the tape roll.

She talks about everything she can remember except her adult life. When I prod her, she grows suspicious and refuses to cooperate.

Twenty minutes after tea, she says it's time for her nap.

"I'd like to arrange another session to…"

"No need, young man. I've told you everything I know."

She asks me to lock her front door on my way out, then goes in the bathroom.

Maybe she's the type who brushes her teeth before her afternoon nap—the way I was trained. *Bad breath can ruin a young man's legal career.* Lunch. Teeth. Nap. *Get in the habit.*

In the bright sunlight outside, it's hard to think of my parents as dead, but not too hard to imagine Roberta in a casket. She practically lives in one already. Once they shut the lid on you, no janitor goes in there to keep the satin clean. The next person to visit your space may be an anthropologist six hundred years from now.

Roberta Joyce. A spinster. Sure. I'll look you up, Roberta, and the spouse you didn't love and the child you despised. Research libraries keep track of all that.

There's nothing like lies and denial to stimulate a nosy genealogist. Next stop: Washington, D.C. The library of the Daughters of the American Revolution, where I spend hours unearthing Roberta's family history from the stacks, and where there's no record of the many relatives she told me about. The family is still numerous, though. A collection of diverging last names. It takes too much work to keep track of them all—a family tree that turned into wild honeysuckle. The sweetness of procreation getting carried away into boring statistics and vital records.

Second marriages were as common in Roberta's grandparents' day as divorces are today. They resulted from the early deaths of first spouses. There's a Thomas Bradford who married a second time—his first wife having died only four months before his second wife had their first child. Thomas had an affair with his second wife while still married to his first. He left his lover pregnant, and when his wife found out, she died of grief, and he promptly married his pregnant sweetheart before the birth of their child.

They lived happily ever after.

These are the types of deductions genealogists draw from a small collection of dates. No one alive today ever met Thomas Bradford, but the dates in his record tell us he was a scoundrel, so we're allowed to tell his story the way we see fit.

A few decades after Thomas, I run into Annabella Joyce, who mesmerizes me. She lived to age ninety-two. Never married. Inherited a gown from her mother. Nothing from her father. And that's her total historical record. Ninety-two years gone in a flash. No one knows anything or can ever know anything about her aside from the inherited gown.

I write her name under a column headed *Barren*.

Hewitt won't mind if I give her a couple of children, and great great grandchildren who died in infancy shortly after her death. Descendants of a purely female line who had nothing to do with the Joyce surname and therefore are of no interest to Hewitt. Annabella deserves that.

I move her name one column to the left and put her down with three daughters. The whole point of genealogy is to make the mortal immortal. In some cases—when the departed leave diaries or journals—that task is impossible. A collection of clichés in a notebook won't earn you any immortality points. Better to burn those diaries late in life and die a mystery than have your great grandchildren laugh at your unremarkable, workaday nonsense.

Actual quote from a diary left by someone named Peter Joyce: "Fine weather today. A bit worm in the mourning, but fine nonetheless. Mammie complained about the heat so I set up a parasol for her and she was grateful. I really wanted to take off my jacket, but it was most improper in the church and everyone was suffering from the heat..."

So it was a hot day on 15 August 1832.

A key piece of information for the future of mankind.

The diary of a weatherman. *Peter Joyce: The Immortal Meteorologist.*

Most diaries are left by military men. With their martial sense of importance and impending death, they describe at length this and that campaign, or how they decimated an enemy and led a successful attack. There are few diaries left by those who lost the battles, and too many by those who take credit for winning them. Too many penned by missionaries and clergymen. Too few, or none, by those you're trying to research.

Aside from Peter, no other Joyce seems to have ever owned a quill or a pen. Three centuries from today, when researchers of the future try to find out more about us, they won't have to worry about a similar lack of material. Our generation will be ever-present to our great great great grandchildren—through thousands of Polaroids, negatives, compact discs, digital photo albums, and email archives. That is, if anyone bothers to carry the digital baggage that long.

Frustrated, I give up on diaries and journals and start compiling Joyce lists. Every Joyce everywhere in the United States.

Brenda Joyce, actress. "She played Jane to Johnny Weissmuller's Tarzan in *Tarzan and the Amazons*, 1945."

She's a dud. Brenda Joyce is her screen name.

Real name: Betty Leabo.

Peggy Hopkins Joyce. Another one who fails the list. Joyce was her married name, from one of her six husbands. She's also in the historical record because of her Hollywood connections. "The movie *Gentlemen Prefer Blondes* was based on her," the source book says. "She was a vamp, a gold digger." No mention of the husband who gave her the Joyce name. Just someone with money.

Female Joyces of the past get lost forever in the family lines of their husbands' surnames. In some cases, those male lines pop up as self-appointed dynasties: Elizabeth Joyce marries John Theodore so-and-so. Their first boy is John Theodore II. Their grandchild John Theodore III, who begets John Theodore IV who sires John Theodore V who begets the sixth. Elizabeth's last name means nothing to the almighty Theodores.

I don't know Gem's last name. I can't even visualize her face. She's not sitting two tables down with pen and paper. No one is. This room is filled with an army of genealogists buried in microfilm projectors. They switch reels and take-up reels with the frantic ticks of those who try to accomplish too much in too little time. Unfulfilled humans toiling endless hours in research libraries, thinking they'll find something special about their genetic pasts before death takes away their futures.

When people die, their bodies start to rot within minutes. Human cells know when it's all over. They turn themselves off, commit suicide, and open the kingdom's gates to the maggots.

But that was not the case with Jesus. *Jesus Lives*, says a bumper sticker outside the library.

The Biology of Jesus. A bestseller waiting to happen. On the back cover, it would say: "Jesus lives, and this is the book that explains the biology behind resurrection."

If I could only write such a book.

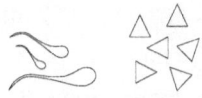

Hewitt loves Roberta's toothbrush. Calls it a gold mine. Everything to him—if it's of any use—is a gold mine.

Gem's a gold mine. She is still being mined in Ireland.

"You have graduated from our genealogical-research boot camp," he tells me. "The toothbrush was your thesis."

And my salary is about to jump.

And my life is about to get interesting.

Hewitt says all this without looking at me. He's multi-tasking, in front of the computer at his conference table, doing research, writing a letter, investing, describing my exciting future.

"Ever been to Zurich?" he asks, and brings up a color animation of grainy bubbles on the screen. "When you cut yourself chopping onions in the kitchen, the cells around the cut start dividing like crazy. Look at them. That's how they cure the wound."

I see bubbles becoming more and more bubbles.

"Protein molecules act as the messengers that tell the cells to divide. Imagine if armies could do that. When the word goes out— *The enemy is coming!*—the King's messengers go to his men and tell them to divide and multiply. An army of fifty becomes an army of six thousand in a matter of seconds."

Hewitt asks me to finish the story.

I draw a blank. What story?

"Make it up, Reed. Be creative. King's men dividing and multiplying. Think of something. Be the writer you say you are."

I thought we were about to discuss my salary increase. My soon-to-be exciting life. Zurich. I've never been to Zurich.

He insists on the King's men's story, and ends up telling it himself. "Here's what happens," he says. "The messengers can't shut up about it and keep on telling the men to divide. Soon, the castle is packed with three-hundred thousand men. They can't all be fed, so everyone dies. End of story."

"There's a moral?"

"Cancer. That's how it operates."

"I can get cancer chopping onions?"

"You can get cancer doing anything," he says. "It's not the doing that's the problem. It's the messengers. We have to teach them when to shut up."

My new salary will be five-thousand dollars every two weeks. He hands me a one-way ticket to Zurich and enough pocket money to get there.

"Someone will meet you at the airport to give you your first paycheck. After a few weeks of additional training, you'll be on your own. We're after Joyce's gene now."

two

Hewitt says James Joyce died—and is buried—in Zurich. There's a team currently working on extracting DNA fragments from Joyce's remains. I'm not part of that team, just going there to learn our subject's historical background in the city.

All this is confidential.

"Consider your salary hush money," Hewitt says. "We're paying you this much to keep the work to yourself. Don't cause any cancers."

Once the project succeeds, *then* I can tell the world about it.

Hewitt is after Joyce's literary gene. His assistants are in the process of taking DNA samples from everyone who might be even remotely related to Joyce. From the samples, he plans to isolate what he calls Joyce's WR125—the writer-genius gene—and find out if the material is cloneable.

"Have you ever read Joyce?" he asks.

If I say No, do I still get the five-thousand?

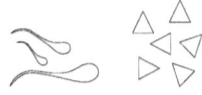

Bipolar-Down Gem picks me up at Zurich Airport.

I'm not surprised.

Ireland, Switzerland—just a plane hop away.

We get in her rental car and drive around for two hours.

It's a tour, she says. This is where Lenin learned how to totally control a population—right before he moved to St. Petersburg to apply the lessons learned.

James Joyce lived here, too, on *Reinhardstrasse*—and on so many other *strasses*, that Gem drives me into motion sickness trying to visit them all.

I don't want any tours.

"This is where the Joyces are buried," she insists. "The internationally known *Irish* writer never lived in Ireland once he was old enough to leave the place."

Write what you know, I guess.

Gem explains Hewitt's plan for a publishing empire based solely on the WR125 gene. It's been mapped already, and our mission is to find out who has it, and then approach those who do and nurture their writing careers. Give them the opportunity to write. Sign them up. Make billions out of them.

"I work for Hewitt just like you do," Gem says.

Sure.

"My duties have more to do with the biological aspects of the project."

We're going up a steep hill, and the little German car is barely making progress. Lake Zurich is behind us. It looks so melancholic, I think of a young orphan at his mother's funeral.

Project Shakespeare, Gem calls it. A mundane name for a brilliant mind like Hewitt's. "It's important not to let the subjects know about the research," she adds. Otherwise, they will take their writing talents—once they find out they have the WR125 gene—to another publisher.

There are no visible hovels or shanties in Zurich. We're a long way from the emerging economies—from the humidity, mud, and lack of symmetry of a place like Rio. At least, poor Brazilians know their homes well: eighty-square-foot warrens made of cardboard, plastic and corrugated iron. They build them themselves.

In Zurich, even the downtrodden have indoor-plumbing, centrally-heated apartments, cable, telephone, and Internet access. They have it all. But do they know anything about what's inside their own walls? Do they understand the technology they use daily?

For Immediate Release: The cantons of Zurich, Schaffhausen and Aargau have officially decreed a new law on personal property. The new code states: "You can't own it if you don't know the science behind it."

From now on, every home built must be delivered with a phonebook-sized manual explaining all the technology in it. You have to learn it all before you can buy your new home, no matter who you are or how much money you have.

All buyers must take a test to show their knowledge before they are allowed to move in.

Every new house must have Lucite wall sections that let you see the wires and pipes inside them. They must have see-through sewer stacks to show you what you're flushing down the toilet, and where it's going.

"Gem, any good discos in town?"

She doesn't respond. I can tell she's tired. Her perfume is wearing off, and she must feel in need of a shower.

"Hot shower," I say. "I picked up some German before my departure. *Ich bin geil.*"

She doesn't care.

We're sharing a room in a low-grade hotel where tourism doesn't get in the way.

Two single beds.

"Aren't there better digs in Zurich?"

"We're trying to save the project some money," she says.

"But that's kind of stupid. I'm making five thousand every two weeks and…"

I shouldn't have said that. Maybe she's making much less than I am. She's a woman, and Hewitt glass-ceilinged her, and I don't want to have to testify in her sexual-discrimination lawsuit.

"Your five thousand won't kick in until you're in Galway," she says.

"Galway?"

"Ireland."

"What for?"

"That's where you'll be doing most of your research."

"You said Joyce never lived in Ireland. Never wrote in Ireland. Why Galway?"

"It's Joyce Country. Cork is where his immediate ancestors came from, but Galway has all the Joyces. We already have what we needed from Joyce himself. Now we need to find out who else has it."

It's a waste of money and time, in my humble opinion, but I'll do it for five thousand every two weeks.

How much are *you* getting paid, Gem?

She says Galway is just a start. The research will take me to Wales, then to Germany, where it is said the Joyce surname lived its ugly infancy spelled *Jorst*.

This could take years.

Thousands of Joyces in Galway alone.

And why stop with Germany? Let's go further back in history, back to the Vikings, Mongols, Neanderthals and oranguhumans. Somewhere in our past, there must have been a monkey who picked up a stick and pretended it was a pencil. *He* was the first literary Joyce. Let's clone *him* and inject his simian genes into Hewitt's publishing extravaganza.

I'm afraid to ask Gem how she feels.

I wait in vain for another manic "Up" episode, like the one at the disco. She seems to be bipolar no more. Just polar. South polar. Frigid and serious.

She takes out peach-colored panties, a matching bra, jeans, a sweater and sneakers. Her suitcase is large enough to hold twenty times that.

While she's in the shower, I stick my hand deep into the suitcase and move it about until I hit something hard. A hardcover book bound in leather. A diary. She must be thinking grandchildren—the only ones who would ever bother to read grandma's daily writing. Gem's a fertile Annabella Joyce with hopes of a husband and progeny.

"My communion is between me and my God" is the first thing I read on page something. "No one else has the right to listen in on our sacred conversations." Dated a couple of months ago.

Is Gem religious?

I time-travel back a few pages. She writes about biology: "Scientists who believe in God are more common than people are led to believe. Most Darwinians are not consummate atheists."

The water stops running in the bathroom. The diary goes back to its cocoon.

In movies and novels, a man and a woman sharing a hotel room must inevitably end up sharing a bed. But it's a sham. Humans are not designed for further sexual attraction once they've ruined a relationship by starting it with a disco sex night.

We're not angels.

She's out of the bathroom.

Perfume and peaches.

I'm browsing a biography of James Joyce she left on the night table.

"Says here Joyce lived in Italy. When are we going?"

Not of interest to us, she says. We're finished with James Joyce.

I don't think so. He lived in Paris, too. "Can't we at least spend a couple of weeks in Paris? There's something there I must see."

She scoffs. "The Eiffel eyesore? The art at the loo? They've been whittled down to nothing by tourists."

"Think less touristy, Gem. Human remains. Bones. Catacombs. Few tourists know about them. A seven-block area below Montparnasse. Bet you've never been."

The Hewitt Publishing Group has just released The Ghoul's Guide to European Ossuaries. *Get a guided tour of the femurs, tibias, and skulls stacked six feet high—the victims of plagues, the guillotine, and the French Revolution.*

A buildup of calcium.

Chapter Two: "The smallpox epidemic of 1418: Fifty thousand corpses in six weeks. And those were just the first batch. As the years passed, another eight hundred cartloads of exhumed human bones joined them from the Cemetery of the Innocents."

Dumped underground.

"Human landfill."

Humanity is nothing but a bone factory gone amok, a factory where production never stops. And as you watch the overstocked inventory, you wonder: What are all the bones for?

And no one has an answer.

The factory keeps on churning out bones because that's the way it is.

Forget Paris, Gem says. Project Shakespeare has clear goals: isolate Joyce's gene and use it in a DNA delivery system. "Remember how you dreaded shots as a child?" she asks.

I don't. Masochists enjoy shots.

"And how sometimes they produced allergic reactions and left a big mark on your arm for the rest of your life?"

That's old news, Gem. Even I know doctors have been using drops for shots ever since soft kids became the parental product of choice.

"Most painless vaccines are expensive and have to be refrigerated," she says, "which makes them even more expensive. Hewitt's solution is to graft them into the DNA of our daily diets—to deliver them to the world gradually, so people don't even know they're being vaccinated."

"Peaches and cream?"

She nods. "Peaches with the polio vaccine in them. Serve the kids some peach ice cream, and eradicate polio forever."

It's almost a shame to see Gem being such an expert. I bet she doesn't know the first thing about reaming toilets. When there's so much biology in your brain, it's hard to leave room for the simpler things in life.

Gem doesn't even fit the expert's role. She looks more like someone who should be in running-shoe commercials. Too much of a forehead to be a beauty queen, but fit and trim. If I were her agent, the first thing I'd do would be to get her to stop pulling her hair back. It's not meant to be stretched and tied against the skull like plastic wrap.

My communion is between me and my God.

It's hard to forget about the God in her diary, so I focus instead on the Goddess in her.

My communion is between me and my Goddess.

There are times when a man can be so in awe of a woman, that it isn't love or lust he feels for her but envy for not *being* her.

Gem's worth ten thousand dollars every two weeks instead of my five. A match for Hewitt.

"James Joyce's biography says he lived in Trieste. Let's go to Italy, Gem. To Venice. No one's ever heard of Trieste. It must not be as romantic as Venice."

Gem's not in a romantic mode.

The Project doesn't have the money.

Her heart doesn't have the heart.

We are in Zurich, and after Zurich comes Dublin.

"Are you ever getting married, Gem?"

I just ask.

She tells me about William Shakespeare's only mention of his wife in his last will and testament: "I give unto my wife my second-best bed."

Nothing else for the woman.

Spouses are not very kind to each other, Gem says. It's too much to ask.

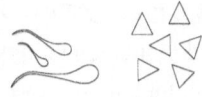

The alarm clock rapes my ears at 5:30 in the morning.

Alarm clock or fire alarm?

Gem's up and ready in five minutes. "We have a plane to catch."

I need more rest.

Last night, after she was safely asleep, I stuck my arm one more time into her suitcase and fished out her diary. I spent a couple of hours reading it in the bathroom.

It's more a notebook than a diary. Too serious. No gossip. No criticism. Mostly God and biology. Nearly every entry with different-color ink.

When a diary snooper sticks his nose in someone else's writing, he has only one goal in mind: finding his name and what is said about him. "Restaurant meal with Reed." My name next to Zurich recipes, of all things. Beer. Potatoes. Cabbage.

"Lunch with Reed at a beer & potatoes restaurant." Just like that. She doesn't even bother with the name of the place but uses the generic. Might as well write *Ate food with man.*

For our disco night, the entry is "Went dancing with Reed."

Not accurate.

I feel like writing a correction: "Danced twenty minutes, made love all night."

Aside from the generic eating and mendacious dancing, I am mentioned nowhere else. A nobody, especially next to God, who makes numerous appearances—not one of them generic.

Hewitt comes in second, listed as "H."

At least there's been no dancing with H., that I can tell. But there is a folded note from Hewitt to Gem. "You are my best asset," it says. "Have I told you I think you have a great genius? That's the honest truth, and I'm not easily impressed by human beings."

"Get up!" Gem sticks her rapist alarm clock in my ears.

Next, I'm having a drink in seat 14A.

Gem hands me my first five-thousand check.

"You can't cash it until you reach Galway."

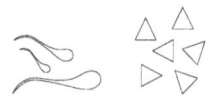

Dublin isn't as kind as Zurich. No hotel room to share. Her apartment is large enough to have a guestroom, where I stay, far from her diary.

The furniture looks intentional, expertly placed where it's supposed to go according to a decorating plan seen in some magazine. Gem says she had nothing to do with it. She likes simplicity. The apartment came furnished.

The kitchen is well supplied with nothing. Gem doesn't cook, and Dublin has a good choice of her favorite: beer-and-potato establishments. Food places where she can eat food with men.

I'm her trainee. As such, I'm to be instructed in the nuances of Project Shakespeare.

"Collecting DNA samples can be a time-consuming activity," she says. "You have to gain your subject's trust first. Be imaginative. Enter a 10K race. Learn the names of your competitors. Any Joyces in the race—get a piece of them somehow. Snot. Saliva. People are careless when they run. Less guarded with their fluids."

Gem is full of ideas.

She proposes I become a part-time worker at a morgue.

Expose myself to body parts and such.

Hairdresser. Hair samples.

Night cleaner at a local hospital. Bio-waste.

Five-thousand every two weeks.

There is still an intellectual part to the project, she insists. Historical and genealogical research must fill at least a third of my time.

"Don't go overboard with bio-data collection. It'll burn you out."

In the bathroom—there's only one in the apartment—her hair is smothering her brush, begging to be part of our Shakespearean experiment. I wrap a few strands in toilet paper and put them in my pocket.

I have several opportunities to read her diary while she's out on errands. It's fruitless reading, however. So impersonal, the entries feel like press releases. Hewitt's biographer will find the material very useful someday—a map to the success of Hewitt's media empire, full of the nuts and bolts, the nuts who took part in Project Shakespeare.

DNA collectors.

Literary scouts.

Assistants to the publisher.

Gem admires Hewitt: "He's a genius and an entrepreneur," the diary says. "A combination that is impossible to find more than once per century."

Before leaving one morning, she hands me a map and a guide. "Here. Learn something about Dublin. Go for a walk. Explore."

She's too busy to give me a tour.

Maybe Hewitt shouldn't have hired me, she says. I'm not curious enough.

But I am. My mind is simply on Galway, on cashing my first five-thousand-dollar check and experiencing the Galway equivalent of Temple Bar, on my own. With Siesta.

My training's not finished yet, Gem says. There's too much to learn.

Everywhere I turn, God figures prominently. Aside from Gem's diary, her Dublin Guide goes into Christ Church Cathedral, Saint Patrick's, Saint Andrews, Whitefriars, Werburgh's, Saint Anne's, Saint Audoen's, Saint Stephen's.

Gem's apartment rests on the site of a thirteenth century Augustinian monastery.

We're surrounded.

"Who is more pious: Church-going Christians or Natural Christians?" Gem asks in her diary. "Church Christians go to church. Natural Christians don't bother. Their church is everywhere. They follow the gospel of Thomas."

I look up Thomas in the massive encyclopedia she keeps on her night table. He's the spurned apostle, the one whose writings were left out of the gospels. He forgot to turn in his manuscript on time.

"Natural Christians ask difficult questions," Gem writes, "while Church Christians merely repeat the words from the choir."

Repeat after me, they say at Saint Patrick's, where we're all on our knees. I've taken Gem's advice and started my tour of Dublin. The topic today at Saint Patrick's is horses. Everyone chants the Psalms:

A horse is a vain hope for deliverance;
Despite all its great strength, it cannot save.

Oliver Cromwell—I read in Gem's guidebook—rode his army into Saint Patrick's Cathedral and turned the church into a stable for his soldiers.

A person cannot mount two horses or bend two bows.

I can imagine the soldiers galloping right in.

"Welcome to Saint Patrick's Equine Shelter, gentlemen."

The horse is made ready for the day of battle;
But victory rests with the Lord.

Saint Vincent de Paul is the Saint of horses. But so are Saint George and Saint Anthony of Padua.

Jonathan Swift took over as dean of the Cathedral in 1713. Then he wrote *Gulliver's Travels*.

We chant the appropriate Psalm:

Sovereign Lord... How can Jacob survive? He is so small!

All of us Lilliputian worshipers look up at Swift's death mask and listen to Handel's *Messiah*. We experience the synergy of beauty, religion and art. We're tourists, Church Christians and Natural Christians—all visiting the Cathedral for different reasons.

"If God allows humans to discover the mystery of DNA, does it mean He wants us to use it as a tool to do more?"

Gem's diary has cloning in mind. "Every human emotion and action—lust, murder, pollution—is part of God's Master Plan."

I hear the front door open and put her diary back.

Gem goes in the kitchen.

"Irish bananas from Africa." She has a bunch in her hand. "Want one?"

A welcome break from beer and potatoes.

"Did you go out?" she asks.

"No. I imagined it all, like a mental tourist. Your guide served me well."

"Stop wasting your time, Reed. There's too much to see here. Bedford Tower. The Book of Armagh and the Book of Durrow at Trinity College. The Genealogical Office. Millions of documents from the past."

I'm not interested. The past isn't past. "When I finish this banana, may I take another?"

"They're all for you."

Gem doesn't like bananas. She attended a parochial school with immaculate nuns. "I was eleven," she says. "At lunchtime one day, I sat on a bench in the yard with a banana."

She peeled it and started to eat it like any normal human being would eat a banana. But a passing nun didn't think so. "Child," she said, "but you look just like an ape, poor thing. It's not proper to eat a banana that way—holding it like that—putting it IN and OUT of your mouth. It's so unholy, so...obscene!"

Gem didn't know what the nun was talking about. She was just eating her lunch. But from that day on, she could never eat a banana without thinking she was doing something dirty.

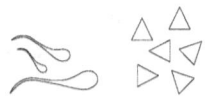

It's the start of my on-the-job training. "Millions of cells are shed daily inside your mouth," Gem says, handing me a packet of cotton-tipped swabs. "Mouth cells contain DNA. Now, follow the instructions."

Open the packet and remove the swabs without touching the cotton.

Gem takes one swab and twirls it on the inside of my cheek.

Use a firm, scraping motion.

I don't see the point. We're not going to stop people in the middle of the street and ask them to open their mouths.

"Never mind," she says. "If you can become an expert cheek-scraping DNA collector with just a few minutes of training, why not?"

"I don't need to become an expert."

"You may need it in Galway."

Galway. *A delight of narrow streets*, says the guidebook, *lined with the world's best pubs and restaurants and most picturesque storefronts fashioned in wood and stone.*

My trip to western Ireland has all the characteristics of a covert operation. I am told to collect DNA samples from unsuspecting guinea humans—something the U.S. Army would do, and admit to only a century later.

Last train to Galway, with the salary of a well-greased operative.

Go West, young gun.

Hardly a gun. I'm more like a sponge, sucking up body fluids from every Joyce I meet.

Galway. *Gateway to Connemara. A heaven for musicians, intellectuals and artists.*

After Galway station, my first stop is the Bank of Ireland, where they turn my five-thousand-dollar check into euros.

Siesta insists we play *Rich Man, Poor Man* with the money. I give in, and pledge to live the first week of our stay in Galway as a Rich Man, spending the whole five thousand in seven days. In Biblical terms, this will be our fat-cow week.

And the cows that were ugly and gaunt ate up the seven sleek, fat cows.

For all we know, Ireland may plunge into a new potato famine six days from today—so it makes sense to live in the present, to spend paper money while money is still worth more than food.

Siesta asks me to hire a limo, hire a driver.

Rich man.

The driver asks me to call him *James*, and he begins a tour of the city with Eyre Square, followed by City Wall, the Spanish Arch, and Lynch Memorial. Then Bowling Green and Nora Joyce's home.

The Finish line will be a suite at The Great Southern Hotel, at $500 a night.

"Don't they have anything more expensive in Galway, James?"

I have to spend it all this week.

If you have money, don't lend it at interest. Rather, give it to someone from whom you won't get it back.

Gem spends her loot on a luxury apartment.

Rich Man Poor Man won't do that.

The whole point of Siesta's game is to experience extremes. Living it up in a millionaire's apartment one week, and starving in it the next—still surrounded by luxury—doesn't qualify.

If the hotel doesn't charge enough, Rich Man spends his money on clothes and gives the suits away to charity at the end of the week.

I buy a Senior Project Manager wool suit. I ask the tailor if he can get me a razor to shave in his bathroom. They'll do anything for you when you buy a high-end suit.

Then we head to The Great Southern, with my new leather suitcase in hand.

I order room service while the international news is on the tube.

Between headlines and mouthfuls of *Wild Mussels à la Galway*, I read *Deep Biology*—a gift from Gem.

Chapter Four says Vikings are special. Their descendants in Iceland tell us that their genes were culled from the rubble of two major plagues and one gigantic volcanic eruption.

One mussel and a sip of white wine.

Switch channels.

More news: Babe Ruth made $80,000 in his top year.

Most Icelanders look eerily alike, the book says. The earthquakes, brimstone and fires of Iceland weeded out genetic diversity. As a result, many on the island today carry the same damaged gene: breast cancer. An ancient mutation.

Babe Ruth didn't know how to play the game. The tube says that a contract just signed with a lucky shortstop will pay the young man 550 million dollars in exchange for ten years as an indentured servant.

There's one mussel left and half the bottle of Irish wine. *Eau de Shamrock.*

The uniqueness of Iceland's Viking genetic pool makes the country a natural lab for genetic research.

The lucky shortstop is twenty one. His name is Cog.

Iceland's population is 272,512. Three-fourths of the country's surface is wasteland.

Cog could give each Icelander a gift of $1,500 from his ten-year contract, and still be left with more than a hundred million dollars.

I'm the Cog of genealogical research. Grossly overpaid. $5,000 every two weeks.

When you come into Cog's kind of money, suddenly you are too good to ream your own toilet. You hire a maid. Upgrade your spouse. Get a new house with new toilets.

Someone on the screen says, "This isn't baseball. The boy's just a cog in a grand marketing scheme—part of the cost of making even bigger money."

Icelanders are so related, the joke goes, their phone books have to be alphabetized by first name.

Cog doesn't care what they call him. He's laughing all the way to the bank. "I've been a cog every day of my life," he tells reporters. "Better a well-lubed cog than a discarded bearing."

Hewitt didn't pick an Icelandic writer for his project. There must be many, famous only in Iceland because they failed to write something like *Ulysses*.

In the morning, I'll have my underwear and socks dry cleaned, just because I can. A rich man's way of helping Galway's economy.

Joyce Scholar Comes to Town, Gives Meaningful Jobs to Local Folk.

It's the duty of the rich to live in luxury in order to give lesser beings something to earn a living from.

Scholar Philanthropist Engages Local Economy.

Mr. Philanthropist wants to do good. He goes into a depressed town and creates a job program for the poor.

But Galway isn't depressed.

Pubs are cheerful places.

I finish my burnt oranges and lemon curd, close the biology book, and surf more news before the phone rings.

Gem's happy to know I'm living it up at The Great Southern. Asks if I have any prospects.

No, but there's a man at the front desk with a name tag that says *Thomas Joyce, employee of the month.* I gave him a tip, even if none was required.

Mr. Joyce didn't check me in. He just stood there. I'll engage him tomorrow.

On The Philanthropy Channel, Peter Bolt, CEO of Monaco Luxury Yachts, Inc., says no human being "should be allowed to live in daily squalor."

Gem wants me to check if Thomas chews gum. Get his saliva.

Not at The Great Southern. Employees wouldn't be allowed vices like that.

"Poor working conditions," says Bolt on the tube, "are the first step to *willful* unemployment, and a downward spiral toward homelessness and unhappiness."

Mr. Bolt is swimming in ignorance, Siesta says. Living conditions don't matter at all once you get used to them. And it doesn't take more than a few days to do so, especially if you're hungry.

My resume is enriched with five and a half months of "Activism for the Homeless." Employer: Global Neighbor (GN).

GN's Mission Statement: "We strive to raise our clients' living standards."

Reality: Standards of living supported by charity never last.

During all of the five and a half months, Siesta kept on revising GN's Mission Statement with what we saw in the grim streets of downtown.

People are poor because life is meaningless, and they just can't cope with that fact.

Jobs like mine at GN can make anyone schizophrenic. Daily journeys from the realm of $400 ergonomic office chairs to the kingdom of stolen shopping carts—rolling closets for junk—and back to networked $3,000 workstations hooked up to the world by DSL and million-dollar contributors.

Given the time, any oranguhuman can learn to ignore his surroundings.

And it takes all of a week to get used to anything.

Rich man.

Poor man.

Every other week.

My pledge to Siesta.

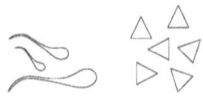

Fiona and Aidan O'Flannigan had a child two months after they got married. The scandal must have brought the village down.

There's nothing about the scandal in the old record book in front of me, or in this entire archive. You look for your subject's name in the index, fill out a request form, and the historian on duty hands you a heavy volume filled with nearly undecipherable handwriting. Bound sheets aged more than three-hundred years.

I sit at a table near the historian's desk. He checks on me every thirty seconds.

Fiona and Aidan were close kin to a few Joyces. But they were sinners—disowned by their families, forced to play One With Time.

When I meet them at the train station, they're amazed by modern mores. "Look, Fiona! Unwed mothers—they get monthly *government* checks!"

A few decades back, Fiona points at a pregnant teenager who's barely in high school. Class of 1956. The girl has several boyfriends—not one of them walking with her in the dark alley on the way to an illegal abortion.

In ancient times, Aidan hears the call in the darkness: "Stoners wanted! Stoners wanted! Good pay. Needed to stone to death unrepentant fornicators—unwed girls under the influence of illicit pregnancies. Stoners wanted! Good pay...."

Somehow, I get hired for the job. I am ready, with the crowd, but there aren't enough stones to go around. Someone tells us to throw the ones we already have, pick them up, and throw them again. "Recycle your stones, citizens! They're a precious commodity."

The teenage sinners try to flee from us. But there's no use.

In the meantime, Fiona and Aidan are rolling in the hay. He's having trouble undoing her dress.

Jesus comes around to scold us. "Stop it with the stones!" he yells. *If any of you is without sin...*

Before he's finished with his message of love, I become Aidan O'Flannigan's hand, making my way under Fiona's dress.

I'm all over the place, and Fiona talks to me in whispers while I adore her. "Is it true that Jesus never had a child?" she asks. "If he was ever a father, he must have thousands of biological descendents among us."

Jesus may have had children who are not mentioned in the Bible—children who had many grandchildren in the missing Book of Roland, which begot the Book of Alfred, which begot the books of Robert and Lester, all the way down to the Book of Modern Times. A New Testament revision every year would help track all those who descended from Jesus, thus keeping the world's growing population active in faith.

New Testament 98.

New Testament 2005.

Upgrade now, or your soul will fail to boot up next year.

Fiona and I are not that advanced. We're still stuck with our abacus, calculating the due date of our love child, while the stones keep on flying at us.

I shield her.

The Courageous Lover.

The Valiant Fornicator.

"Don't stone us," I whisper to the angry crowd. "Jesus is *you*. Our love child is not a beta version. He's your brother."

But stones are a powerful drug. The crowd is addicted.

I see Fiona O'Flannigan lame, black and blue and in tears.

When all else fails, make the most out of your wounds, Fiona.

There will soon be a crowd gathered, with a pastor telling the faithful, "Let us pray, for poor Fiona O'Flannigan, who was made lame by a savage mob...let us pray."

"Let us gloat, too, because sinners always get what's coming to them. And for poor Aidan O'Flannigan, who is no longer with us..."

One stone too many.

The love child is fatherless.

Fiona needs a new man in her life, and she finds one in Alberto Eufemio Ignacio Joyce, the son of a Spanish mother and Galway father. His mother came to Galway with her wealthy merchant father. She found herself a Joyce, and they had *Albertito*.

I include the story of Aidan—minus the Biblical aphorisms—in my research notes, which I make up as I go, for Gem's benefit, and Hewitt's.

Alberto Eufemio Ignacio Joyce is a composite, and not too far-fetched. At one time, there were enough Spaniards living in Galway to have annual Spanish parades. Let Alberto marry Fiona the Lame. Let her live. What does Hewitt care?

I rush back to The Great Southern to check out by noon.

My first paycheck has run its course. The suits and leather suitcase go to charity on Augustine Street. Everything else, except what

I'm wearing and the DNA kit, goes in the trash. And I keep Siesta, of course. And we rent a room—or more accurately, a bed in a room—in a flophouse in a neighborhood where the streets have no names.

The landlord is a smart man. He lives on the premises, in the same squalor as the rest of us. No one begrudges him ownership of the building.

"Skip the fourth step on your way up," he says. "It's rotten."

I pay him the week's rent in advance. The equivalent of less than a meal at The Great Southern. There's enough left in my pocket for some careful grocery shopping.

I share the room with three other men.

Metal bunk beds with thin, smelly mattresses.

No formal introductions. Just a glare from one. A burp from another. And a "Make yourself at home" from the third.

They're all on the dole.

I wish I'd kept the suits to line the filthy mattress.

At least I won't freeze to death here. There may be no light in the room, but a massive radiator, sunk in the rotting floorboards next to the window, keeps the place like a sauna. In this heat, I can sleep in the nude, without covers, though not with these roommates.

The radiator gurgles like a leaky toilet tank. Terry, the friendly make-yourself-at-home guy, catches me staring at it in the dim hallway light.

"Not as bad as it looks," he says. "Or you'd rather be in the rain outside?"

Terry has freckles and light orange hair. He soon starts sharing his most intimate feelings—how he hates Africans and all the asylum seekers and refugees who're "turning Ireland into a shit soup."

After five minutes of racial evisceration, I tell him I was born in Africa. He's perplexed, and I let him hang there a moment before I explain: "My dad was an oil worker with an American company in Nigeria. It was a tough life."

Terry punches the air above him. "I knew it! Can't be an African without the tar skin, man."

I go out into the dismal Irish mist and find a corner store with Siesta still under my arm, inside a plastic bag. Can't leave her with Terry and his lily-white pals. They might rape her.

The menu for the next couple of days: a pot of raspberry jam, small bars of chocolate, a large loaf of bread, and two African bananas.

Plastic knife and spoon on the house.

Cheapest tabloid to use as toilet paper.

Once my basic physical needs are covered, I need to take care of my mind with a public-library stop on the way to the flophouse. If I hold a book up all the time, maybe Terry will spare me his social engineering plans.

Public libraries are the average hobo's salvation.

Mission #45: Global Neighbor strives to get library cards for all its clients.

All the clients who live at the flophouse are watching television downstairs when I return. I go to bed in the dark, hide the food under Siesta, and place the books in a pile next to me.

Lean Cow Poor Man.

The toilet down the hall has *never* been reamed.

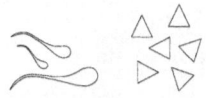

Wake-up call in the middle of the night: noisy lovemaking right under me. Terry and somebody. Every piece of metal in the bunk bed joins the symphony of grunts and muffled screams.

I'm on the bed of a truck, riding along a dirt road full of pot-holes. Got to clutch my pot of jam in case it rolls from under Siesta and crashes somewhere.

First thing I see when I look down in the morning: a used con-dom on the floor.

Terry's awake. Alone and smoking a cigarette.

"Sorry if we woke you," he says. "Sometimes, I get an itch for a whore in the middle of the night. Won't happen more than five nights a week. Promise."

"She African?" I ask.

Terry turns red. "You little fucker...you think I'm into bestial-ity?"

"Then why the condom? Who needs protection from the perfect race?"

"*He's* the imperfect one," his lover answers for him. She's back from a trip to the toilet, wearing a large, stained tee shirt as a night-gown. "I'm the one into bestiality, shagging this animal. I'm Ruth. Need me services too, dear?"

"I do!" yells the Burper from the top of the other bunk.

Ruth is already half dressed and says she only has five minutes, tops. "Close your eyes, boys."

While Ruth and the Burper make the other bunk rattle, Terry lights another cigarette. "Fucking brasser," he says. "Doesn't make *him* wear a condom."

"Shut up, Terry." The third man is up now, staring at the couple. "Everyone knows you have fucking gonorrhea and who knows what fucking else."

I pretend to go back to sleep, but can't do it for long. I ask Terry where I can find a job around here. Is there an employment office?

"What do you want a job for? Go on the dole. We're all fucking government artists here."

Foreigners can't suckle at Mother Ireland's tax breasts, I explain.

"Go back to Africa, then. Don't they have a dole there? I swear, that's why we have so many tar monkeys seeking asylum all over Erin—for a piece of our Irish dole."

The Burper's five minutes are up.

Ruth rushes out. "Just pay me at the end of the week."

Her clients are honest and pay off their sex accounts on time.

Terry and the Burper start arguing about who owes Ruth more money. I open the covers of James Joyce's *Finnegans Wake*. Published in 1939. "Joyce's final masterpiece," says the blurb.

The third man is out of the room. I'm not getting up until Terry and the Burper leave.

Finnegans. You know you're in for a scholarly read when a novel has a forty-page introduction by someone other than the author, plus ninety small-print pages of endnotes.

Skip the introduction.

It takes me twenty minutes to read page one of the actual novel.

And I don't understand any of it. My Internet-trained brain doesn't have the neurons for this. My Saturday-morning-TV-cartoon childhood didn't prepare me for it.

Total confusion.

What's Hewitt up to, I wonder, trying to market *this* guy's writing gene? Literature that requires hallucinatory mushrooms to understand it may be the fruit of genius, but it can also be the fruit of a joker.

Here, readers! I'm famous now. Try to read THIS crap!

I jump to page somewhere: words that no one has ever seen in any dictionary. Hundreds of made-up words.

And it goes on. Hundreds of pages filled with word salads, all dressed in non-grammatical vinaigrette.

"You're wrong, Terry," the Burper yells. "I fucked her *six* times last week, so I'm up *three* on you!"

Someday, right before this building meets the wrecking ball, an audio archeologist will listen in on this friendly discussion. When Terry says, "Fuck *you*, man!" his words vibrate on the room's walls. The walls act as a cassette tape for the stream of electromagnetic waves produced by his voice. All you have to do is play back the tape—the walls—and listen, when the right technology to do so is developed.

Scientists are already using a variation of this approach with Rembrandt's paintings. With every coat of paint the master put on a canvass, his words—spoken while he painted—were frozen in the pigments. Hewitt claims to be working on this as a "side project." His plan is to lift saliva from old paintings, from the pages of manuscripts, from furniture—anything known to have belonged to some artistic master. All grist for his patented, hand-held scanners that suck up human particles from the past.

Hewitt is obsessed with the past while living far away in the technological future. It's all a race to new discoveries for him. And so it is for me, though at a different pace and historical zone.

Today, I discover that this is as far as my James Joyce scholar career goes. Leave the word salads to dedicated vegetarians.

"Hey! That's *my* name," Terry says. He's pointing at *Finnegans*. "Joyce, man. Terry Joyce."

The Burper is finally gone. I'm alone in a room in a flophouse with my first prospective DNA sample.

"Terry Joyce, man. I'm blue blood in this town. Joyce Country. I own the fucking place."

I offer him the book. "They say it's good, but I'm having a hard time with it."

Terry's not interested. He doesn't read, he says. Just watches TV.

Do you have, like, hundreds of cousins, Terry?

He does. He's my DNA gold mine. Five-thousand dollars every two weeks just to get to know this guy and his relatives. Visit them all. Go in their bathrooms with my DNA kit. A cinch.

"I happen to be working on a family-tree project of the Joyce family," I say. "Maybe you can help me out."

"No problem, but I have to take a piss now."

I wait, alone in the room. I imagine that all sorts of *fuck you*'s are bouncing back at me from the walls. But they're just coming from the dining room downstairs. The Burper's having a pleasant breakfast chat with his fellow flophousers.

Finnegans goes back on the library pile. The Excellent Prospects pile.

Next volume in line—*Michael Collins, Irish Hero: The Life & Times of the Irish George Washington*.

One of my high-school teachers always said that heroic acts were a matter of historical perspective. If George Washington and Michael Collins were young men today, they'd be in prison. Condemned traitors. George on death row.

"History often makes heroes out of criminals," my teacher said. "Let some time pass, and a terrorist can become an honorable terrorist. A traitor can grow into a patriot. Democracy can justify sabotage and murder, can justify Lexington and Concord, can justify Bunker Hill."

It's 1775 and there's taxation without representation, and you are a young colonist unhappy with the Redcoats. What do you do? Turn their children into orphans. Make their wives taste grief.

Go to Concord, young man. It's a patriotic stampede.

Blow a few Reds up. It's all for a good cause.

Then flip the calendar's pages to the 2000s. You a young American unhappy with the Feds, with taxation full of misinformation?

Just try blowing *anything* up.

They'll call it "domestic terrorism."

You'll get death row.

Lethal injection.

Eternal hatred from all souls.

Face it, young, unhappy Americans. The *George & Michael Show* is no longer favored by the ratings. Acts of treason are justifiable only when committed long in the past, and when the traitor's side has won.

It's all a matter of perspective.

I wait, and Terry doesn't come back.

Guess he's not going to make his bed, pick up his clothes, or throw away the used condom.

I have to think about this a moment. Amateur rapists don't wear condoms. They leave their semen in their victims' bodies, like business cards. The police take the cards to the lab, and the rapists get busted. Off to rapist jail, where rapists get fitfully raped every hour.

It takes me ten seconds to stick a swab inside the condom and be back on my bed as if nothing happened.

Prepare the DNA kit for mailing to Dublin. A note to Gem: "Hope this is useful. Joyce semen. Don't ask me how I got it. More DNA to come, not necessarily in this format."

A day's work well done.

Sit back and relax.

Breakfast in bed.

Open the pot of jam. It's warm and sweet. I eat it by the spoonful. The label says *Refrigerate after opening*. But this isn't The Great Southern, with a small fridge in every room. Everything is warm here. Siesta is warm, too. The room smells like sweaty loins, and the windows don't open.

Home, sweet home.

After breakfast, I take a long walk to the post office and mail the DNA kit to Dublin.

"Handle With Care," says the envelope.

Terry's inner child on a swab.

The racist gene.

Same as the jingo-nationalist gene.

Same as the honorable terrorist gene.

I realize I'm stuck with Terry now. A DNA sample by itself is of no use to Hewitt. Terry must be placed on a relational family map, become part of a database with the names of his parents, siblings, cousins, bastard children. I will need to get samples from as many of them as possible.

Their DNA, once analyzed, may turn up some interesting discoveries. I can elaborate and fictionalize some of the data and produce a potential bestseller: *Washington, Jefferson and the Irish Connection: How America Owes its Independence to the Irish.*

The ensuing controversy alone would make the book a bestseller. So I immediately produce another: *How the Irish Won America's Civil War*, which sells and sells because Irish yarn books are always in fashion. I'm on a roll with a third installment: *My Horrible Horrible Horrible Childhood in Cork.* The story of a family of twelve with extremely hungry children. Nothing to eat but beer. And another: *My Great Great Grandfather's Potato Famine Exploits.* A variation on the Don Juan story—a charming man with a cellar full of food to give out to the local lasses in exchange for services rendered.

My Struggles in the Troubles. Terrorist turned honorable terrorist tells all.

Milk the genre till the udder's destroyed.

Be a son-of-a-gun dairy writer.

How to Write Irish: Step by Step Guide to Produce Your Own Bestseller in the Genre. Chapter Two: "Most importantly, avoid facts. A good yarn's a good yarn. Just add a bit of the Irish and wait for success: Six million copies in hardcover. Twenty-two million in soft. Hollywood is interested. After the movie, they make it a game show, followed by a sequel, action figures, toys, lunch boxes, tee shirts and diapers."

The problem with earning too much from one's writing is that money turns into distraction and comfort, and both kill the discipline required for additional, meaningful writing.

A dilemma of the first order.

At the other end of the scale, however, starvation walks give me plenty of ideas but no energy to put them on paper. There's nowhere to write in the flophouse anyway. I try a library. A pub. A phone booth. No luck.

I sit in a café where they loan you newspapers. Scandal rags that don't require much reading. Like a child, oblivious to the news of the world, I look at the pictures. They're big and colorful "privacy busters" of the grainy celebrities they claim to portray. One of them gives the photographer the finger. *Fuck YOU!* says the caption.

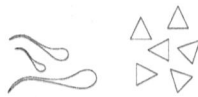

Terry invites me to eat with his mother.

"It's O.K. She doesn't like Africans, but you don't look like one anyway."

His idea is to enjoy dinner, have a good time. Then, at the end of the evening, spring the news on her: "Mum, Reed is African." See how she reacts. "Hope she doesn't have some kind of attack."

I'm game.

"Just don't contradict her," he says.

In her living room, we can barely hear each other. Mrs. Joyce has been losing her hearing and needs top volume on her television set. She smokes a pipe. "It was my late husband's," she says. "Got to keep the tradition."

"What tradition is that?" Terry asks. "Lung cancer?"

"Don't pay attention to him," she tells me. "My husband died of emphysema. It's not the same thing."

Then, relatives start materializing.

Sister with spouse. Two children.

Brother and girlfriend.

Cousins. Uncles.

Full house.

"Terry, I thought we were just having dinner with your mother."

"Surprise! You said you were studying the Joyces. Well, here they are."

Terry's already drunk. He asks his mother to bring me "the package." It's a bulky mass wrapped in butcher's paper held together by a long string.

"I need them back, son. But find out if they're valuable." The package contains family letters, she explains. "They've been read only once."

The roar from the relatives and television is too much. I seek refuge in the bathroom and wish I had an Irish family-size DNA kit. With so many people, I have to get organized.

The bathroom's too dirty to imagine only the old lady uses it. A sample from it might end up not being accurate.

I came prepared, though, with nail clippers small enough to hide in my hand. I just have to practice. Snap. Snap.

Wave my hand close enough to my head. Snap. A hair.

Back at the table, with Irish stew already served, I'm the night's attraction. Everyone's asking me questions. "Where you from, Reed?"

I look at Terry.

"He's from all over. Hasn't lived in any one place all his life."

Mrs. Joyce tells the clan about how I'm studying the family.

"No skeletons in *my* closet," one son says.

Blah, blah, blah. Just shut up and give me your samples.

Most Jacks of all trades are all business—their minds always impatient for that next job, a new trade. They don't want to waste time with what they're doing. Just get it done, professionally, quickly, and go on to something else.

"We have a cousin in jail," Terry says. "Incest with a donkey."

Everyone gets the chuckles.

Terry's sister, Mary, jabs me with her fork. "Do you know the one about the half-wit obsessed with marrying his auntie?"

More laughter.

I miss the joke.

Maybe there's a lot of inbreeding in this gang, on purpose. Family tree turned electrical post—short a few wires.

"The donkey turned out to be an ass!" someone yells.

Ha ha ha ha ha. They're having the time of their lives.

I run my hand past Mary's laughing shoulder. Snap. When I see her hair in my fingers, I excuse myself.

In the bathroom, I label the sample. Wrap it in toilet paper. Put it in my pocket.

Next.

By the time we get back to the flophouse, I have enough hairs to make a wig. Hope Mrs. Joyce doesn't mind that she ran out of toilet paper.

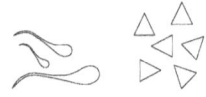

Mrs. Joyce's meat-packaged letters turn out to be nothing. Two years of mundane correspondence—mostly love letters from the now dead Mr. Joyce to his then sweetheart and future pipe-smoking wife. Embarrassing. If I could scan old saliva off the pages, maybe they'd be of use.

"Damn, Reed! We forgot to tell her you're African!"

Terry is in a drunken stupor in the lower bunk. Ruth is on top of him. He's catching up with the Burper.

Four more days of this, then back to The Great Southern. Pledge living can get as tiring as constant luxury, especially if your living companions are striving non-achievers on the dole. Pledge traveling is a better proposition. Unless you are a nomad, it's not a permanent condition. You know it has an end.

How to Be a Pledge Traveler. "Chapter Seven: God-fearing churchgoers pledge how much they'll give to their church during their lives in order to buy their salvation. A Pledge Traveler operates under the same principle. Though instead of pledging to give, she pledges to spend—as little as possible."

As a bestseller, the book will brainwash readers into impulsively taking Pledge Trips.

> *Trip #1: Pledge to explore the United States of America for a period of three months, spending no more than five dollars a day. Start in Houlton, Maine. End in Fairbanks, Alaska. In the middle of winter. Never spend the night within twenty miles of where you spent the last one.*
>
> *Pledge to always be on the move, like a fugitive, and to never take a trip unless it's one way. The most dissatisfying part of traveling is going back to where you started.*
>
> *Pledge to support yourself by doing any job that will pay you those five dollars a day. Don't earn a penny more.*

The librarian seems to be fascinated with me. She's never seen a Joyce scholar sorting hairs on pieces of toilet paper on one of her research tables. I bet she's related to Terry.

Chances of any resident in Galway being related to another? Very high. If we go back far enough, even she and I could find a common ancestor.

On a lone piece of toilet paper, I deposit one of my hairs.

Throw Gem a challenge.

Hewitt's money will tell me how close I am to Terry and his family's totem pole.

Maybe I'll wave my hand past the librarian's head on my way out. Find out who's playing *her* piano.

The piano is an analogy used by some scientists to describe the A, T, G, and C bases of the genetic code. Each base is represented by several piano keys, they say. We're all born with the same piano, so what really matters in life is the piano player. A beautiful melody represents the perfect, healthy life. No mutations. But if some jerk is banging on your keys, you're riddled with cancer.

I learned this at Genotype Corporation, where I worked six months, four days, and two hours. Started as a technical assistant in charge of washing lab equipment. Scientists get very upset when test tubes sit in an autoclave. They need a wife to pull the things out the moment the washing cycle is done. I was the wife, married by a paycheck to a host of nasty husbands always complaining about the dishes being in the dishwasher. My job was to keep the place spotless, like a four-star restaurant where stains on the silverware are a capital crime.

Genotype was into primate research. The company went through monkeys like a football stadium goes through hotdogs on game day. Two of the test animals were treated almost as house pets, however. A pair of siblings called Mono and Mona. They were used for the less lethal experiments.

I quickly worked my way up from dishwasher to assistant to the project assistant. The promotion came with a fractional pay raise. I bought Mono and Mona a bag of peanuts to celebrate.

Siesta spent her days in fits of jealousy while, at the lab, my bosses and I made history by inserting a fluorescent gene from a jellyfish into one of Mona's unfertilized eggs. Then the chief scientist used Mono's sperm to fertilize the egg, and Mona carried the experiment to term.

Artificial Monkey Glows in the Dark!

We worked well together until the chief scientist fired me for "embezzling" six dollars' worth of lab equipment: three pairs of colorful earplugs that we used during experiments. Test monkeys can get pretty loud when you don't use chloroform. Earplugs are essential if you want to keep your sanity. I needed the earplugs, but shouldn't have taken them without permission.

Genotype didn't make my resume. I kept the earplugs, though. And if I had a pair of them now, I'd use them to block Ruth and Terry out, Ruth and the Burper, and Ruth and the Third Man who never says anything.

The post office is open. Note to Gem: *I'm truly out of money now. Last package to Dublin.* Signed: "The Hairdresser. We do perms, bobs, shingles, bouffants and, when nothing else works, we shear."

I'll be forced to borrow money from Terry.

Three more days.

I'm thirty blocks from the flophouse. Two blocks from The Great Southern. It's freezing.

Toasty in Ireland: The Backpacker's Guide to Where to Warm Up in Winter. Every page would contain a list of churches—hearths for limbs and soul. *Toasty in Finland. Toasty in Russia. Toasty in New Zealand.*

The *Toasty* series. Known the world over.

I warm up on a back pew, reading religious pamphlets. "The cost of publication," says one, "has been generously given in the form of a Memorial to Elizabeth Lynch, a granddaughter of former rector Lynch."

I close my eyes and imagine being Elizabeth, warming up her pew, keeping her faith.

"Elizabeth Lynch worked for our congregation all of her long and useful life," the pamphlet says. According to the dates listed, she spent seventy years as a pew warmer in this church. Certainly a long time, Siesta says. But was it really useful?

Gregor Mendel, the monk who also found time to experiment with genetics in his monastery's garden—mixing religion with science—spent a useful life in his church. In the eyes of God, who was more useful: Elizabeth or Gregor?

"Scientists who believe in God are more common than people are led to believe," Gem wrote in her diary. I could use that theme in a novel: *The Formula*—the story of a brilliant mathematician who spends his life working on an algorithm that can explain or deny Creation. "There's no more true believer than the one who doubts and spends his life searching for proof," Gem wrote.

If I put my mind to it, I could write, too.

When Elizabeth's pew is warm enough, I go back in the cold.

There's a *Help Wanted* ad on a window on my way to the flophouse.

A restaurant.

I talk to the surly manager. He asks me if I have any experience.

Thinking of Genotype...Yes, of course. "You'll never see cleaner dishes after I'm finished with them."

Three days as a dishwasher, and I work like an animal. I lend *Terry* some money when he runs out of cigarettes and condoms.

The restaurant hires the usual crowd of people who hate their jobs. It takes them but two hours to start hating me, too, especially after I tell one of them to be happy in her work. She immediately runs to tell the others about it. "That new American arsehole—had the nerve to tell me..."

How to Be Happy in Your Work. Chapter One: "The first week, be a dynamo. Second week, a dynamo. Third week, a double dynamo. Amaze everyone with your positive attitude and zest for life."

At the restaurant, I make three co-workers superfluous in two days. I feel the condensed, super-concentrated resentment towards me from them, just because I'm striving in my new job.

They glare.

They spit.

"We had a perfect non-productive routine going here until you American arsehole came to piss on it."

I give the restaurant's owner a business idea: Open a store in the empty space next door. Call it the *Croûtonnerie Pain Vieux*. Put a sign up: "Croutons in 163 flavors. Sold in bulk. Garlic. Cinnamon. Mango. Anchovy. Or any customized flavor." Don't throw away the restaurant's used bread. Make a profit.

Chapter Six: "Be happy in your work. Don't waste your time working if you're not going to do the job like a master. Give your employer your best for as long as you can stand it. Then move on."

As the cliché goes, there's nothing like hard physical work for the creative writer. I stack the plates on the counter. Give them a rinse. Put them on the rack.

Most writers can't write during Fat Cow. It takes a dishwasher job to recover from the shock of Great Southern living.

Steam. Rack. Lemony soap.

Write what you know, rich man-poor man.

How to Deal With Personal Financial Collapse.

Fat cow, starving cow.

Sell what you experience.

The Flophouse Guide: Europe on a Frayed Shoestring.

Three days out. The manager is no longer surly and wants me to stay when I tell him I need a week off. He says he's never seen anyone as reliable as I am, so experienced and efficient. I could easily make assistant manager in five, four, *two* months—if I don't take a week off now.

The current assistant manager is standing right there, unhappy in her work, as pink as a pink slip, thinking: *American arsehole.*

"No, thanks. I need my week off." I write The Great Southern's phone number down for the manager. "Give me a call if one of the regulars doesn't make a shift. I'd rather do that."

Hewitt's second installment is already in my pocket. On my way out, I walk around the building and enter the restaurant through the front door.

The assistant manager drops her jaw.

Dinner for one, I tell her. It's early, but customers are coming in behind me and she doesn't have time to go to the kitchen to tell the others.

More customers come in.

Basket of bread. Butter and wine. It's a long wait.

Outside, a woman arrives in a compact car and checks her face repeatedly in the rearview mirror. She doesn't seem to like her hair and plays with it this way and that.

When she gets out of the car, I notice she's wearing a leather skirt and a silk blouse under her heavy fur coat. Flowers in hand, she waits for someone.

Member of Parliament and Secretary in Secret Love Affair. Cumpton Denies Involvement With Young Aide.

The woman waits for her lover while I wait for my food. She stands on the other side of the window next to my table. The restaurant's neon sign produces a shadow under her mountainous cheekbones.

Red roses made white by the light's hue.

Neon gas glows red when ionized with high voltage. "Exciting a low-pressure gas," they call it in the industry.

I spent two weeks as a neon-light maker's apprentice.

It's not on my resume.

The assistant manager is talking to the manager at the other end of the room, probably wondering how I'm going to pay for the bottle of *1958 Eau de Shamrock* with the nothing I made working here.

My steaming-hot coddle arrives, while the expectant lover must be freezing out there. I can see her breath, and she can see the steam coming up from my food. Somehow, it makes me feel guilty. But she has flowers with her, and flowers indicate love, and when you are in love, things like freezing weather don't affect you.

No Member of Parliament arrives, however. Instead, a woman joins her, a woman half her age.

The roses crash on the pavement.

There's a slap. An insult. A punch. Then flying fur and screams.

People gather around to urge them on.

When blood starts to trickle under their noses, all I can think of is going out there to take DNA samples. What gene makes people hate with such passion?

Suddenly, a man steps in. An aged Member-of-Parliament type in a heavy coat and sweatpants. He talks to the younger woman as he takes her by the arm. I can hear his voice as it bounces on the thin glass. "Leave your mother alone," he says.

Meanwhile, the lover remains on the ground, bleeding from the nose. Nothing left of her fur coat.

The man leads the young fighter away. The spectators, under red neon-shine, jump to help the wounded animal. Someone says the man who stopped the fight is the girl's father—and the woman on the ground, his ex-wife.

I walk to The Great Southern and feel more than ready for luxury.

"Same room, sir?" they ask.

Maximum Luxury Monk. The story of a murderer who gets to serve his life term in a comfortable cell. The victims' families file a lawsuit to keep him from serving in luxury: *Why should this criminal live a comfortable life? Put him to death, like he put his victims.*

During the appeal, his supporters demonstrate outside the courthouse: "Killing is wrong," say their signs, "no matter who does the killing."

"Capital punishment—a crime like any other."

In *Monk*, the novel, there would be a twist: laws are passed to abolish the death penalty. But as a compromise, the victims' families are made to pay for the cost of maintaining a killer in prison for life. That way, *they* decide the level of comfort the criminal gets. They are contractually obligated to pay, but they can choose to pay the minimum—to provide the killer with the bare basics: a clean cell, water, meals, and a cot. Nothing else. No TV. No cigarettes. No sugar. No gum. No fun. They turn the killer into a monk. They are responsible for killing the killer instinct in him.

Another option: The court could give killers the choice of lethal injection or serving humanity by becoming guinea humans in space exploration.

That approach could backfire, of course. Inside a rocket on his way to Mars, the murderer could become an overnight global hero. *Live, from Mars! Space legend Peter Hauser has reached the Red Planet and performed several scientific tasks that will be of immeasurable benefit to mankind.*

Victims would become mere historical footnotes:

[1] *Mr. Hauser caused the intentional but regrettable deaths of twenty-one people before he became an astronaut.*

My luxury-monk experience includes a relaxing bubble bath that gets interrupted by Gem's phone call.

"Where have you been?" she asks.

"Working, of course. Didn't you get Terry's sample? And the wig? Soon I'll have Terry's family tree charted and on its way to Dublin. Maybe I can even take it there myself."

Gem doesn't want to see me, she says. She wants me to stay busy—and in touch. Hewitt has been trying to contact me for days now. If he's paying my salary, he's got to be able to find me wherever I am.

I don't argue, but the flophouse doesn't have a phone.

The more annoyed Gem sounds on the phone, the more I want to see her. Those nights in Zurich come as a dream now. Our proximity. The shower. Her diary.

"I want you to stay in the hotel tomorrow," she says. "Byron wants to talk to you."

I notice that. *Byron*, not *Hewitt*.

"I'll be in and out, Gem. Have a research meeting with a historian at the archive. Already scheduled. Can't change it."

**

The phone rings again at 2:30 in the morning. Someone imitating Donald Duck, asking for Daisy.

I hang up.

Forty minutes later, another call. "This is King Al-Hussein," the voice says in phony Arabenglish. "It has been brought to my attention that your next archeological dig interferes with my ancestors."

I hang up after the voice says he wants to speak to King Tut.

And the night is ruined. I can't go back to sleep. Siesta proposes a couple of hours of One With Time to cure the insomnia. Walk to the window. Open the curtain. Put on a shirt. Close the curtain.

Undo. Repeat.

Redo. Unpeat.

One With Time.

One With Gem, who doesn't want to see me. I open the curtain and realize she doesn't have to. I can see *her*, in the morning. My fake meeting with the historian at the archive is my excuse for taking an early train to Dublin. I never said the meeting was at an archive in Galway.

Since this is Fat Cow, I purchase Premier tickets.

In Dublin, I play private investigator.

How to Write Authentic Potboilers. "The self-help guide every aspiring writer must own. Author Reed Lodge shows us how to successfully produce *film noire* on paper." Chapter Four: "The key is the heavy use of sarcasm. Don't be afraid to pile it on."

I try my hand at the style while I wait for Gem to come out of her building: "I wait for the broad to come out of her building and keep an eye on the scene from a café table across the street. Sketch what I see on my reporter's pad like a storyboard for a major motion picture. *La Donna.* Italian-Irish co-production. Vicious female Mafia boss (la Donna) sets up shop in Dublin while hiding from her former Calabrese associates."

Reed, a down-and-out Irish poet, gets hired to track her every move.

The boys from Calabria are ready to order a hit.

"Make it look like an accident, boys. You know, cracked head from a hit-and-run by some Irish drunk."

I'm their man in Dublin.

Drinking my pint.

La Donna gets cancelled the moment I see Gem emerge in a light-green cardigan, red skirt, and leather boots. An easy target to follow.

I'm on her trail.

An empty mesh bag hangs from her shoulder. She must be on her way to the market.

But her first stop is a hotel.

I wait five minutes. Ten. Fourteen. She comes out with a man. Someone her age, much more threatening than Hewitt.

Traffic and people make following them difficult. Dublin is booming and *Blooming* with tourists. I almost lose them, but stop worrying when I see they're on their way back to Temple Bar, to Gem's apartment.

I should call her. Interrupt whatever it is they're doing or going to do. Pretend I'm Donald Duck. Do *something* to stop them.

But it's not long before she leaves her building again, by herself. I could ring her doorbell and talk to the man. Find out who he is. But my instinct tells me to go after her.

The mesh bag still hangs from her shoulder. We walk several blocks before she enters a four-story office building.

I get closer and read *Medical Offices* on the entrance door. First thought: Gem's selling her eggs. That's what enterprising young women do these days. Lupron shots in their stomachs to shut down their ovaries, then Metrodin shots to force their bodies into hormonal overdrive. The resulting eggs ripen like seeds in a grapefruit. Suck them out with a needle. Good money, they say.

Too much hassle and pain, though, especially with what she must be receiving from Hewitt every two weeks. Fat, fat cow.

Egg-selling wouldn't explain the man in her apartment, either. Unless he's a client who's purchasing eggs.

But if that were the case, the man's wife would be tagging along, making sure Gem's eggs are fertilized in vitro, on a petri dish, and not in utero, with his very active participation.

I forget the egg business when she comes out of the building, a bunch of bananas in the mesh bag. She's going to tell the man her nun story. Must be one of her seduction tools. It worked with me.

I run on a side street to make it to her building before her. Wait in hiding across the street. And there she comes, walking calmly with her load. Four, five, six bananas, at least.

Where can you get bananas in a four-story building with doctors' offices and no produce market in sight?

An hour goes by before the man leaves by himself.

Then Gem, walking in my direction, to my café.

I ask for the back door and, in less than ten minutes, our roles are reversed. Gem sits at a table with a cup of coffee, her eyes on the street, though she's not looking at me.

I could join her, but the café's owner might say something like "Another cup, sir?" Gem wouldn't be pleased.

A young man walks in and Gem stands. She's all smiles. They shake hands. *How are you doing, Sean? Hi, Gem.*

I'd like to know what they're saying.

How do you like your eggs, Sean? Poached? Sunnyside up?

Off they go to her apartment. And I can't stand the sight.

Hasty retreat to Galway and Siesta.

**

Bomb scare at Heuston Station. Train delayed.

While I wait, I look for an excuse to come back to Dublin. Check all the Joyces listed in the phone book, and start calling. Like a telemarketer, I rush through a list of reasons why they should talk to me. But nobody bites. Everyone's tired, eating dinner, or watching TV.

When I'm about to give up, somebody's butler answers the phone with rare formality. "Yes, Mr. Joyce might be interested in talking to you," the man says. "He is a genealogist himself, overseeing the clan's coat of arms, in fact. He is *The* Joyce."

When The Joyce finally comes on the line, my train is announced. He goes on and on about his qualifications and pedigree. "You are a Joyce, as well?"

"No. Just doing genealogical research on the surname."

"Oh. Mormon."

"No. No religion's involved. I'm a certified genealogist."

The Joyce calls his assistant to take notes. He asks me to spell the name of the organization that issued my certification and a phone number where he can get in touch with them. I give him their website. He can see my name there. Member in good standing. Paid my dues—the several hours of boredom.

"We don't get our fingers dirty with the Internet," The Joyce says. "My assistant shall research the matter. I have to make sure you are a legitimate researcher before I meet with you. I hope you understand."

I make Galway past bedtime, with a wad of bills still in my pocket. There's a pub. I ask for a pint and a phone book. My heart needs musical therapy. Gem's running around, telling nun anecdotes to hundreds of men. Music will help me deal with it. I look under *Recording Studios*. Get a pack of cigarettes. Another pint.

No Love Tonight. I write the lyrics on a napkin. A Dublin-inspired torch song.

I was in love...
You had your plans.

Bad lyrics deserve to be put to music, recorded for posterity.

You did me wrong...
I did you right.

Torch the torch song, Siesta says, then put out the fire with a couple of pints.

I don't listen. *Brandon's Mike.* Recording studio, by the hour. Fourteen blocks from The Great Southern. Open 24/7, or "Whenever You're Feeling Creative."

I am now. Another pint, please. To go.

Brandon's has no sound engineer to speak of. It's a low-budget studio, and that's OK. I tell Sam, the janitor in charge of the place, that I'm just like him, a jack of all trades—session musician, songwriter, promoter, rock star. I'll do it all.

"But let me start with a guitar," I tell him. He and his two lager-drinking buddies can take turns playing all the other instruments. "Just keep the volume up so I can't hear myself going crazy."

The studio's all-digital. One computer, a zillion tracks. Any recording artist can become internationally famous here, following a very simple to-do list: Perform. Record. Produce. Post-produce. Rip. Burn. MP3. Upload.

Fans and Internet retailers take care of the rest.

"Technology has changed everything," Sam says. "The next Beatles won't even have a record label. It'll be just four guys making music in a studio like this one, hiring a marketing whiz to make them famous even before their music is out."

The whiz comes up with the band's name—The Robber Barons—and takes care of their first sensational news release: *The Robber Barons, the emerging band soon to be as famous as The Beatles, has kidnapped Francis Lorton, the steel magnate whose family is worth billions. The Barons demand no ransom other than to have their music videos played on all network television stations 24/7 for a full month.*

A simple publicity stunt.

The emerging Fab Four go to jail for a while, but the world's listening, playing, and singing their songs.

"We didn't mean to kidnap the poor old bastard. Our promoter made us do it. Anyway, thanks for buying our music."

And the next band in line has to top that.

Members of "Shady Monster" Will Jump Off Empire State Building, Guitars in Hand.

The music world is transfixed.

"Shady Monster" Drummer Has Problems with Chute, Lands Splat on Pavement.

"Got any old guitars I can buy, Sam?"

Brandon's has a few. Sam says I can use any of them. They come with the fee.

He doesn't understand. This is not just a recording session. I have my napkin with my lyrics, and my several pints. This isn't music. It's an experience. "I need more than just to play the guitar. I need to own it. How does two hundred sound for that old Fender?"

Sam takes the money.

Violence, by itself, is a godsend. It drains you of all your anger and beer. I pretend I'm a spoiled rock star. There's a sharp corner at the edge of the table. To start the session, I fly-swat it with the Fender.

Sam's not upset. He's seen this before. A case of the splinters. "Totally unplugged, man."

"Are you recording it, Sam? That's the intro. The fatal riff."

I finish the instrument off. Reed the Heavy Metal rocker, smashing his guitar Gem on the stage as a form of therapy.

And the fans go wild.

Cities around the world should harness human violence and use it to heal the psychic wounds of urban life. They should open Main Street stores with padded floors and walls and wire-meshed windows where aggression is not only allowed but encouraged. *The Anger Room*: Rented or subsidized by City Hall by the hour. Well worth the public investment. Any violent man can go in it—by himself—and spend his surplus energy and anger shouting, kicking and punching. Done daily, it can turn into a part-time job for the average gang member. The storefronts can have a slot where passersby can drop bills and coins. The angriest man gets the most money out of his audience. *Anger Room Amsterdam. Anger Room Chicago. Anger Room New Delhi.*

Rome. Bangkok. Pretoria.

Let violence pay.

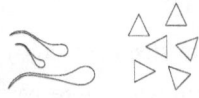

Three in the morning and Napoleon Bonaparte's on the phone asking if I brushed my teeth before going to bed.

"Yes, I did, Emperor." I play along.

"What brand of toothpaste did you use?"

I wonder if the real Napoleon ever brushed his teeth. There were better things to worry about in 1812.

Suddenly, the phony French accent switches to Donald Duck.

"Reed, aren't you wondering?"

I don't wonder when I'm half asleep.

"It's me, Hewitt."

Hewitt the genius, impersonating Disney characters in the middle of the night. MacArthur grant recipient. Cecil J. Rhodes scholar. Scientist and inventor.

"It's this new device I've been perfecting," he says. "Changes your voice to any kind of character or accent you want."

Nothing new, Byron. I had one of those as a kid.

"But this is different," he says. "It allows you to digitally sample a voice—any voice. Say you have a boss you dislike. You can go in his office, sample his voice without his knowledge, then use it to record your own words using his voice. Call the accounting office, say. *Effective immediately, Reed gets a salary increase of one-thousand a week. Make it retroactive to last year.* It works!"

Hewitt's in good spirits, so I ask him what Gem's up to.

"No idea," he says. "She got her instructions. I trust her to be doing her work, just as I trust you to be doing yours. How's the data coming along? Are you doing any writing?"

I don't know. I just want to go back to sleep and enjoy my four-star hotel room. Truth is, I'm getting bored with the research. I think of nothing but Gem. Dream of her taking weekend trips to Galway, just to keep me going with this boring work.

Hewitt's voice drifts off while I imagine Gem as my wife. In an old-fashioned way, it's our first night together after our wedding. I'm in the bathroom, alone, fascinated by her things—her hand lotion, nail file, ponytail holder, bottle of Cutex—items I've never seen before in my bathroom.

Hewitt says he's sampled Alfred Hitchcock. "It's a classic. Listen to this."

Be kind to ghosts. And whatever you do, don't scream when you see one.

"Did that scare you? I also have Orson Welles."

A celebrity from the forgotten past. I wrote to Orson Welles once, when I worked at a diet-shake emporium called *To Your Health*. My boss was trying to turn it into a brand-name California franchise. We sent letters to all fat movie stars and Hollywood notables who might want to drink the diet shake—free of charge. The idea was to impress them with how well it worked, and get them to become our spokespersons.

Hewitt is as happy as a child, playing excerpts from *The War of the Worlds*, *The Magnificent Ambersons*, and *Citizen Kane*.

I was in charge of writing the copy for the diet-shake brochures: *How can a rail-thin actor play a female Sumo wrestler after six months of stuffing her face with ice cream, then go back to her former bantam weight once production wraps? Answer:* To Your Health *shakes!*

The company had a lot of promise. I even invested in it.

Then the news hit the electrons: *Movie Star Sues Studio Over Obesity. Female Buddha Role "Too Demanding"*.

Her weight never went back to normal after the movie, even with a year's supply of our free shakes.

The only thing that went down was the value of our stock.

The woman kept on *gaining* weight.

"Do you want to hear my Lou Costello routine?" Hewitt insists.

I hang up on him.

Maybe my next $5,000 paycheck won't come now. Maybe I'm free.

I turn the light on.

Can't go back to sleep.

I go to the bathroom and lift the toilet lid. I'm at Lou Costello's funeral. Toilet lid up like the lid on his casket. It's 1959. Real name of the deceased: Louis Francis Cristillo. I close the bathroom door.

Bud Abbott is here, too, paying his respects. He's not supposed to die until 1974.

I walk to my bed and greet the other notables at the funeral.

Stooges.

Chaplin.

The Marxes.

I sit on Siesta and I'm Abbott. Sullen. Bitter. Lou and I had not been a team for a while. But people are talking about us, saying Lou was the important half of the act—that I was always replaceable. Naturally, when I hear that, I'm pissed. I walk back to the bathroom and open the door to more 1959: The San Francisco Giants are naming Candlestick Park. Everyone's talking about *Some Like it Hot*, the movie, released just a few weeks after Costello's exit.

Lift the toilet lid. I'm Abbott, on my own. Pissing and pissed. I lower the lid. The young Dalai Lama is escaping to India.

I walk out. Close the door while Hitchcock goes *Psycho*. It's 1960. Orson Welles is drying out. I move back a few months and see the first Barbie dolls going on sale. Alaska becomes No. 49. The world stands at 3 billion people. I keep going back. Bed. Bathroom. Toilet. Bed. Bathroom. Toilet. One. With. Time.

There's a gorgeous glow in the room as I travel.

By the time I'm Thomas Jefferson at the Second Continental Congress, I'm too exhausted to open the bathroom door again. Benjamin Franklin, who's sitting next to me, says, "You're a sight, Tom. Go back to bed. We'll never finish this Revolution business if we don't get enough sleep."

It's a *genetic* Revolution, Ben. You don't understand. Someone's been messing with my genes.

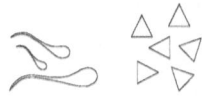

In the morning, Siesta tells me to board a bus.

May the road rise to meet you.

Galway to Mayo. Sligo and Leitrim.

I hitchhike between buses, but only when drivers don't look like respectable murderers.

Fermanagh, Cavan, Longford and Westmeath.

Breakfast in Belfast. Breakfast in Dungannon. Breakfast in Ardee. Final destination: Dublin. Gem.

I stay in the *Princess Grace* room at the Shelbourne. The room has a brand-new mini-refrigerator, put there especially for Americans who like their beer cold. I test the refrigerator's hinges for a few hours, then pour myself a drink.

Room service at three in the morning.

Leftover creamed potatoes. Irish soda bread and any kind of microwaved fish that can be served without bones. For dessert, I ask if they have any Irish bananas.

The Joyce's butler returns my call before dawn. Yes, he says, the keeper of the Joyce clan will meet with me. "The assistant has done the research, sir, and has determined that you are a legitimate genealogist. However, The Joyce must turn down your dinner invitation at the Shelbourne, sir. He has documents and books that might be of interest to you, so it would be better to meet at his estate."

The Joyce's estate turns out to be more of a state of mind. Rather than thousands of acres outside Dublin, it's a few thousand square feet just north of the Liffey River. But money does appear to have gone through the place, at least once.

Earlsfort, it says on the iron gate smothered by ivy. The butler walks me through several sets of entrance doors—more wrought iron, oak, mahogany and glass—into a sitting room with upholstered walls and marine paintings like the ones at Dr. Hurt's.

This is the type of Joyce I should have mingled with all along. An intellectual interested in literature. I bet Hewitt didn't get anything useful out of Terry's semen. But this—it's what Project Shakespeare really needs: the literary Joyce gene, feeding on culture, sculptures and paintings, fine furniture, and a whole wall of books facing an Edwardian desk with three chairs.

I know that my being here qualifies as plundering Gem's territory, but honesty is more important than respecting a co-worker's turf. I've figured my salary to be over a dollar a minute. To deserve it, I should at least get Hewitt one valuable DNA sample. And this is it.

I earn another eighteen dollars before the butler shows up again with a tray loaded with glasses and plates. "The Joyce asked me to offer you a few pleasures while you wait, sir."

How thoughtful. It won't be hard for me to get what I need from my host if we're eating.

"A few slices of Gorgonzola," the butler says, "with home-baked biscuits and a glass of Burgundy."

I eat all the biscuits and drink three glasses of wine while I wait for The Joyce to join me. Fifteen. Twenty. Forty minutes. No show. I don't even know what we're going to talk about. The passage of time makes me lose interest.

There's a large grandfather clock in one corner of the room. It breathes insolently every time I look at it. And when my host finally arrives, its glass shows me his reflection as he enters the room.

"Don't get up," The Joyce says. "I shall sit down to meet you at your level." He is no more than sixty but walks slowly and with the aid of a cane. "Sorry for the delay. I was taking an incredibly pleasant nap and told Harrison not to disturb me."

"That's quite alright, Mr. Joyce. I have all the time in the world."

"Well, I don't, so let us go to the point. Ask me what you need from me." The Joyce emphasizes every word with a mechanical jerk of his body as he takes his seat.

I don't know what I want from him other than a DNA sample. Hewitt's mandate is such, that I have lost all intellectual curiosity about Project Shakespeare. "I work with a team of professional genealogists," I explain. "We're mapping the American Joyce Line, and the European, with the goal of linking the two to generate a world map of literary heritage."

"Literary?"

"James Joyce is our focus. Who is related to him. Who isn't. Who is close..."

"You are another one of those—what do they call them?—literary groupies. I should have known."

"Our research is strictly scientific, Mr. Joyce."

"Well, you've failed. I am *The* Joyce, the keeper of the Clan. By now you should have learned that. Harrison!"

His yelling the butler's name comes with a few drops of spittle, but I'm unable to take a sample.

"Dublin is not a literary theme park, Mr.—what did you say your name was?"

"Lodge. Reed Lodge."

"Mr. Lodge, Dublin suffers through what we call Bloom Idiots, James Joyce tourists who descend on the city every June to do the circuit and pretend that life can mirror a book. I believe you have the same problem in America with Hemingway. Key West, is it?"

The butler is standing in front of us. "You called, sir?"

"Harrison, show this gentleman out. Good day, Mr. Lodge."

I take a slice of Gorgonzola and follow Harrison. Humiliation from *The* Joyce doesn't faze me. It's nothing next to rejection from Gem.

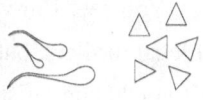

Gem doesn't come out of her building until my fourth cup of coffee. She visits the post, a bakery, and the same medical office where she got the bananas. This time, she takes the bananas to a park, where a young woman is waiting for her. They greet with a fleeting hug, like lovers who haven't seen each other in ages and don't want the intimacy of the past. The woman is petite and tightly wrapped in a pastel dress that goes down to her knees. A pleasant spring outfit. Corporate gear for an executive on holiday.

They sit on a bench and talk. The day is so colorful, I see the two of them as Edwardian women on the canvas of an impressionist painting. They're my subjects. I am the painter.

Painting doesn't pay much as a career, but I tried it once. It's not an activity you measure with time. Only a pompous-ass artist would say, "I've been painting for thirty-two years." The real unit of measure is the canvas—the product. To deal with that reality, a pompous-ass artist will also say, "I've painted six hundred seventy-two portraits, forty-five landscapes, and one still-life." But that's like collecting vintage soda-bottle caps: all hobby, no craft.

Gem and Petite eat the bananas.

Wannabe writers are the perfect pompous-ass artists. You bump into them at most parties. They always say they're working on a book—one they never finish. Siesta makes a point of asking them how many of their books are available for purchase.

"Well...I've been writing for twenty-eight years!" comes one man's reply.

I understand, but that's not what I asked you. Where can I BUY your writing?

"Uh...nothing's actually available yet. You see, I'm vice president at this law firm...trying my hand at legal thrillers, but the market is glutted. I love legal thrillers, don't you? John Grisham's my hero."

John who?

A John approaches Gem and Petite. It's all obviously arranged. They shake hands. Gem seems frail next to his towering frame. An emaciated woman in her nineties, being shaken by his handshake. John the Giant. The good-looking jock with the winning smile.

They chitchat. *Hi. My name is... Yes. Ha ha ha. Ho ho ho.* Nervous laughter that's so thick, it begins to brown the bananas.

Petite laughs herself out of the picture. No longer the *ménage à trois*, I follow the two lovebirds to Gem's apartment, where she must have more bananas.

I should put a stop to this. Jump on them like a highwayman demanding my share of their happiness. But John the Giant turns into Fred the Lizard, Joe the Huckster, Alfred the Librarian. So many men, I can't keep up with the made-up names that identify them. Gem's going through a crowd. They come and go in droves. By the time Sean the Civil Servant leaves her building, I can't resist approaching him.

"How did it go?" I ask.

He seems surprised for a moment, then looks at me as if we were both in the same uniform. "Alright, I guess. She seemed a bit cold and tired. Not much of a session. Easy money, if you ask me."

Then he's sorry he has to leave all of a sudden. "Got another meeting." Jumps in a taxi. Gone.

Not much of a session. The kind of thing bored musicians might say after the band's drummer hits the pavement at two hundred miles an hour. Jammed.

Easy money.

Five thousand dollars every two weeks.

Go back to Galway, Reed. You're not wanted here.

Stop the train, I'm leaving...

May the rail track rise to meet me.

And until we meet again...

**

The train is full and I'm in a seat next to a large woman with very heavy breathing.

Every breath sounds like her last.

The Purposeful Dietist. The story of a handsome man—me—out to do good in the world. Maybe not a bestseller, but a successful little title at health-food stores, at least.

My source material—sitting next to me—is opening a candy bar.

I call her Mindy, and I'm Paul.

Paul the trim and handsome do-gooder realizes that the large woman sitting next to him is a perfect opportunity. He turns to her and says: *Those are my favorite candy bars.*

Mindy smiles. She finds one in her purse and gives it to him.

They strike a conversation, share their likes and dislikes. Paul is careful to pick out her interests and present them as his own. They have so much in common! Weight is never mentioned.

By the time the train reaches the station, Paul asks Mindy out. The courtship lasts several months and, when Mindy tires of waiting for him to propose, she does so herself.

Paul says yes, in a flash, but with one condition: she must lose two hundred pounds.

Then the story gets stuck. I have the strange feeling that it's been written before, maybe even published. If Mindy agrees, she can lose the two hundred pounds, only to find out that Paul doesn't really love her. It was all an act of charity, he tells her. *You were killing yourself, and the only way you'd ever lose weight was if you did it for love.*

Soap Opera Station.

So I set you up to give you the incentive. And it worked!

The Purposeful Dietist. Movie of the week.

Now I must take my charity to someone else in need.

The charitable Paul. Not a very likable character.

Mindy's crushed. Eats her way out of her depression.

Back to square one.

And here she is, to my right, opening another candy bar.

That's the problem with literature. Every story has been told before. Modern writers have to come up with more and more unusual situations to feel they're being original. They turn into purveyors of Drastic Fiction, based-on-a-true-story stuff that sounds anything but true. *Litera-vérité.*

Mindy shouldn't be offered a choice when she proposes marriage. I can make Paul a diet anarchist. A slim activist. An S.O.B. Instead of telling her to lose the two hundred pounds, he kidnaps her and chains her to a bed in an abandoned farmhouse in a remote Italian village—in Tuscany, since books set in Tuscany are always in fashion.

My Tuscan Plan.

Paul visits her for exactly fifteen minutes every day, mostly to scream at her: "It's NOT a glandular problem, Mindy. You're FAT because you're a PIG! And I'll show you."

Mindy's in tears. "I love me just the way I am," she says.

La Bella Figura.

"It's not a matter of love, Mindy. I'm going to teach you what's good for you. You and all the porkers of this world will benefit from my charity."

He serves her what he calls a healthy diet—*a rightful amount*—during the fifteen minutes of shouting. "In times of famine," he says, "there's no obesity to be found anywhere in the world. Doesn't that tell you something, Mindy?"

Sob, sob, sob—to the S.O.B.

"Diabetes, Mindy—it's not a disease. It's only a genetic modification that does very well during famines, and very poorly when it's a constant feast. Insulin is only required in industrial quantities when you eat industrial amounts."

Paul is full of biology and chemistry.

Doctor Jack the Slimmer. Eighty million copies sold.

"By the time you go back to society, Mindy, you'll be a raging beauty. A perfect, proportionate 110 pounds to your five-foot frame. A normal heart running at seventy-two beats per minute. An example to the world. I'll marry you shortly before your triumphal return. Then, we'll tell everyone about our wonderful honeymoon in Italy."

The Tuscan Slimmist. Selected by book clubs everywhere.

"During our six-month honeymoon," says the author on a live TV interview, "we lived on love and water—*d'amour et d'eau fraîche.*"

The audience goes *ooooooh.* Everyone imagines daily sexual marathons. And Paul the author takes the opportunistic opportunity to plug his forthcoming book: *Shed Pounds Through Creative Sexual Positions.*

"We're working on it," Mindy tells the audience.

Everyone laughs.

When we reach Galway, my source material collects her things and gets off the train still carrying her full weight, plus five candy bars. Paul will never happen for her.

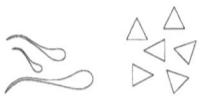

My last morning of Great Southern opulence this week ends with a pot of raspberry jam in bed while watching the news. Maybe there'll be a report on Gem, found murdered somewhere in Dublin. One of her Johns. Or are we talking Seans?

Because random acts of violence are so hard to accept as truly random, we always console ourselves by thinking the victim had it coming to her. You don't just get murdered for the hell of it. You have to be doing something you aren't supposed to, like taking strangers to your apartment. No victim is blameless.

I have enough money left from this week to carry me through the next lean-cow week without having to resort to a flophouse and the likes of Terry.

The classifieds section is full of "Room to Let" ads. *Female looking for female to share apartment. Female needed to share… Female to share…*

Men don't share. Men are not trusted to share.

"Long- and short-term boarding." That's what I need. Regular hours. A set schedule. Eat at the dining room when they call me. Spend the rest of the time holed up in my room—reading, writing, and looking for work. I don't care how much Hewitt pays me. I've had enough of his project and don't plan to do any more work on it. I'll simply send Gem DNA samples of everyone I meet—all the lodgers at the boarding house, the local grocer, the man sweeping the street, cats, dogs.

Mrs. West, the woman who runs the boarding house, is in her seventies. She must have followed the Tuscan diet all her life. As thin as a supermodel on a hunger strike. Dinner portions must be meager here.

"No," she says about meals. "This is no bed and breakfast. We serve no food here. It's a B&N. Bed and *Nothing*."

She laughs at my expense.

"But the ad said *Boarding House*."

"That's just the name, dear. I have to attract lodgers somehow. Once they're within my reach, they're here to stay."

Mrs. West says I shouldn't expect my room to be very warm. Her arthritis is awful, and it's difficult for her to survive the winter months because of it. Every bone in her body aches. But economizing in heating is more important to her than relieving arthritic pain. And did I know she has an unmarried granddaughter?

My room is cold, as promised, and the bed soft and moldy, like peat in the shade. There's a fireplace with a handwritten sign on it: *Don't Use Me*. A large upholstered seat and a desk and chair compete in crowding the room.

When Mrs. West finally leaves, I turn to the employment classifieds. The *Irish Independent*, National Edition. "Biggest Daily in Ireland."

Bricklayers wanted. Crane drivers. Experienced pipe layers. Tunnellers. Plasterers. Shuttering carpenters. Butcher apprentice.

Been there, done everything. Just give me a challenge, a job with a very difficult boss.

"Health Food Store Assistant."

That intrigues me. Nothing could be more difficult than a food crank for a boss. "No animal-products lovers need apply," the ad says. "Meat is murder."

On my way to the interview, the public library has enough books on health-food fads to teach me the right lingo in about half an hour. It's important to impress a new boss with the vocabulary of the trade. I can name-drop book titles like *Veganomics*, *Organic Bounty*, and *Frankenfoods: the Upcoming Plague*.

The store is called Picture of Health. The boss, Monica, is one herself. For the interview, we sit at a table near the deli amid wafts of herbs and perfume and *No Smoking* signs. Monica is a ponytailed, teenage-looking beauty who's probably forty. She's German, she says, and came to Ireland to escape Germany's industrial complex. Her pores were getting clogged with Teutonic pollution.

There's a full-page ad from an American health magazine taped to the wall. *Why do health insurance companies ask you whether you smoke instead of what you eat?* "An odd thing to see in a country like Ireland," I say.

"No," she corrects me. "Healthy eating is a global issue. The ad makes that point. If you have a bad diet, it doesn't matter where you go or where you live. Cancer will always find you."

Whatever. I'll take the job just because I like her. Monica's beauty is deep. Gem may speak several languages, but Monica knows food far beyond vaccine-laced bananas.

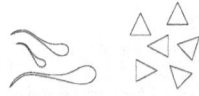

Since Bed & Nothing offers nothing to eat, my source of meals is Picture of Health. I spend twelve, fourteen hours a day satisfying Monica's every whim. I catch her staring at me every once in a while, with a face that says, *Where did he come from, this wonder-boy employee?*

Do as the boss does, and everything will be OK.

While I stock the shelves with cans of organic potatoes, Mindy's five candy bars on the train are still on my mind—my literary mind:

The Supermarket Client. The story of an overweight cashier who pays special attention to one of the store's customers. He comes in for groceries every other day, and she secretly writes down everything he buys, and soon starts buying the very same items. Her motivation is that the customer is the best-looking human being she's ever seen. *If I eat the way he does*, she thinks... Plain oats. Kale. Brown rice. She follows his diet much like the uneducated secretary who invests in the same stocks owned by her successful boss, ending up a millionaire herself by the time she retires.

I start writing at night, and Monica and Picture of Health become such a strong influence, I don't change a thing in my life when I receive the next five thousand from Hewitt.

Stay with Mrs. West.

Direct my energies to Picture of Health.

Make Monica happy—and forget Gem.

I organize the store's storage room so that the inventory moves efficiently from boxes to shelves. I tell the organic farmers to use a separate door for their deliveries to improve the traffic of goods. I reorganize Monica's accounting system so she can better plan her orders and not run out of cash every week.

As a result, she loves me, but that's not why I'm doing this. Office romance? Not a chance. My challenge is to act like her as much as I can. I'm a diet chameleon. A full-blown health nut. Everything Monica says, I follow—at least while I'm in the store. During work hours, I'm the consummate non-smoking teetotaler. No coffee. No tea. Not even the herbal tea that Picture of Health sells. "That's for lapsed naturalists," Monica says. "Don't buy *anything* packaged, even if we sell it."

So I don't.

All my meals are organic, macrobiotic, non-processed concoctions prepared especially for me by Mo, as some of her most loyal customers call her.

It's fair to say the other employees are beginning to hate me, particularly those I've made super superfluous and who are about to get the sack. Mo's not firing them in an economizing, common-sense move, though. Her justification for firing someone is that they're not nature-conscious enough. "They have *meat* written all over themselves," she says. "They *disgust* me."

She's not a very good judge of dietetic honesty, then. If she could read me as well as the others, she'd see not only meat but cigarettes and booze all through my veins. My room at Mrs. West's is like a liquor store of empty miniature bottles. I go on starvation walks every night to have a few smokes before binging at the Irish McDonald's on Shop Street, where you can get green beer with your burger. The same McDonald's Monica pickets on weekends while I manage her store.

"I'm sorry you're an American," she says after one of her vegan protests. The ink on her sign runs down and drips with the rain. *Meat Equals Anthrax*, the sign says. *Milk Equals Cow Piss. Imperial America is chemical-poisoning the guts of the world.*

She has signs like that on the store's windows, as well. And one that says *Vegan Americans Welcome*. She's obsessed with America. "A nation of cocky, greedy capitalists," she says, "who need regular thrashings to keep them from killing everyone else."

I'm not supposed to take offense. I'm different, she says. Not like the rest. Didn't my grandparents come from Europe? Don't I love the environment?

She's very sure of herself.

In her office, there's a large couch that doubles as her bed. Monica the monk lives with nothing in order to spare Mother Earth. "Minimalism is the only thing that can save us," she says. "If you buy nothing—only the bare essentials—you're in peace with the world and the animals."

"That's very limiting, Monica. If you don't buy, you don't experience. Experience equals being alive. Do you think God made television so no one would buy TV sets? If you're part of creation, you have to go with the flow."

"I didn't know you were so religious," she says. "That's another American fault—all those evangelists and TV preachers you have in your country. They're trying to import their phony churches to Germany—everywhere. They're a plague."

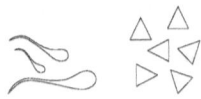

Mrs. West corners me on the landing to ask me personal questions. It's Friday night and all the lodgers are out. We're alone. Would you fancy something to eat? she says. A chicken sandwich?

Her part of the building is impeccable, decorated like a true Bed & Breakfast. Framed sepia photographs of a young woman riding a horse everywhere.

"That was me," she says. "I belonged to the riding club and entered every competition there ever was."

All shared food is just an excuse to socialize. But she doesn't share the chicken sandwich. Only one plate comes—for me. Boiled chicken swimming in mayonnaise between two thin slices of bread.

"My favorite son, Gwilym, died at eleven. My husband, of course, he's been dead longer. But I keep him alive in my memory. This house was his before we married. I have so much history here, and it's all going to end who knows where when I go."

She's the curator of her own family museum. In the collection, there's a wooden box with her late husband's teeth in it. Baby teeth he lost at age six, the ones the tooth fairy kindly exchanged for token gifts.

I ask her if there are any Joyces in her family.

"Oh, heaps of them. My sister married one. Of course, they're all dead now. And they had no children."

I've opened her genealogical Pandora's box, and no one can put a stop to the stream of documents she's dusting out of drawers and cabinets. One is a photograph of her sister, who "died in a hurry." Burst appendix. Emergency room. Funeral. No time to make her wishes known.

"When you die like that," Mrs. West says, "it's like being taken to a party against your will, with a man you didn't want to be with in the first place. You don't have a good dress to wear, or jewelry to go with it, or a drop of makeup. The timing is all wrong."

We go over old photos of her husband, a starched-collar aristocrat who left her just enough money to make her life difficult. But she doesn't complain. If it weren't for the Bed & Nothing, she'd have little to live for aside from organizing her heirlooms.

She has tried to donate her archive to museums, but no one's interested. "People don't care about the past anymore. Young men— they're so *futuristic* these days, with little plastic phones in their pockets and concealed music they take everywhere. So much distraction, they don't have time to think about their parents at all...."

Mrs. West gives me the same lecture old folks have been giving since the beginning of time: *Young people are so useless now, nothing like we used to be when we were young.*

"You bet I wasn't going to let modern times get to my son that way," she says. "I wouldn't have him ignoring his ancestry. We have pure Welsh blood in us, you know. Gwilym was going to be a traditional gentleman."

It seems the unmarried granddaughter is Mrs. West's only surviving heir, but I gather the girl's not up to speed with the world.

"She has her unique features," Mrs. West says, showing me a photo of a woman clutching a purse as if she were about to get mugged.

"Do you think she's attractive?" she asks.

What, to a mugger?

I take a bite of my sandwich, and it drips a large gob of mayonnaise on the lace tablecloth.

Mrs. West is mortally wounded.

"Look what you've done! Grease marks like that don't come off!"

Suddenly, I am little Gwilym, being properly raised by ancient Welsh standards of conduct and duty.

You don't sully the family's honor with grease stains on the clan's lace, you little moron!

While Mrs. West frantically moves everything off the table, we hear a lodger come in downstairs.

"You must leave," she says. "You mustn't be seen here by anyone!"

I go humbly to my room. Grounded. No dinner. No dessert. My chicken sandwich probably in the trash by now. It makes me wonder what little Gwilym died of—extreme discipline, verbal abuse, ancestral overdose, suicide? *Dofydd* rest his Welsh soul.

I empty a couple of miniature bottles.

Siesta is shivering on the bed.

There's a stack of month-old newspapers on the floor next to the fireplace. I collected them from other lodgers, thinking I would defy the handwritten note and have a fire one night. But it never happened. And I'm afraid to make one now. Mrs. West might think I'm trying to burn down her B&N, her family's museum, which is sure to meet the wrecking ball the moment she expires anyway—to make room for progress, for the youthful young men with cell phones and wires attached to their brains.

With the chicken taste still in my mouth, I know it's time to leave Picture of Health to my resume. I have enough money saved to take a few weeks off—to do some brainless thinking. It isn't sloth to lie in bed all day with nothing but your thoughts. It isn't a sin or a vice. It's nutrition for the mind, a holiday for the nerves.

I have to get myself fired. Otherwise, Monica will never let me go. Nor will Mrs. West evict me if I don't do something little Gwilym would never have dared to.

Newspaper balls are a marvel of combustion. I start making them the size of tennis balls—then softballs. Pile them up in the forbidden fireplace. I rip a sheet from a thick weekend edition and see the word "Writers" stand out from an ad.

Get paid for your writing. Read your work to me. — Gem...

And there's her address, the same address I used to send Terry's semen and his family's hair samples.

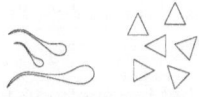

My first conscious act of insubordination at Monica's temple of health consists of leaving an empty fast-food bag on the counter, right next to a crate of organic tomatoes. Free advertising for a fast-food giant.

Do you want chips with that?

I see Monica looking around when she finds it. She's furious, and tears the bag to pieces before trashing it outside. No hamburger grease is ever going to contaminate her store.

Next time, I write on the bag: *Organic tomatoes. Great on hamburgers!* An arrow pointing from the bag to the big red ones.

I take my two hamburgers and chips to a table. Three tables down, there are two pale Picture of Healthers in leather sandals. Leather requires no animal testing—just animal killing. They're having the falafel-and-bean combo.

I spread out my feast: Chips, fried to a fine crisp. Two jumbo burgers that I douse with ketchup from little environmentally unfriendly plastic bags. The unmistakable smell of slightly rotten meat and onions rises from the buns. It doesn't mean the meat is rotten. Burgers just smell how they smell.

"Vat is deez?"

Monica speaking. Anger makes her accent flare up.

"I need some animal protein," I say. "Please. You've been working me to death. I have to *eat*."

I'm a puppy-eyed puppy. Master Monica, please, don't take my juicy bone away.

"*Schweinhund!*" she yells. "Pig dog! You filthy pig dog!"

I've never seen her so red. She unfurls a long banner of paper towel, grabs the whole of my Cheery Meal with it, and out the door. Toxic waste.

"How *could* you?" She doesn't care that her shouting is distressing the falafel eaters. "You are fired. You're fired right NOW!"

She opens the windows. Opens the doors. Must let the herbs and patchouli regain their aromatic supremacy.

I apologize, but it makes no difference. Her senses don't register my existence anymore. Her new accounting system. The delivery scheme. The store's fabulous efficiency—nothing I've accomplished is relevant to her if it has anything to do with meat. Food sinners don't get a second chance.

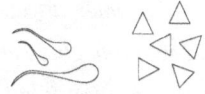

Although I was sure the last five thousand from Hewitt would be the very last, another wire transfer comes, and I feel like an Ivy League boy starting a new semester. Pocket money for fraternity living. Take Peggy Sue out to the drive-in. Get her drunk and buy her some roses.

I withdraw a few thousand euros in small bills for petty cash. My hands still smell like hamburger grease as I recount the stacks in front of the teller. She seems amazed that I would prolong the display of so much cash by taking the time to count each stack three times.

I have the feeling this *will* be the last wire transfer from Hewitt, so I take a bus to Dublin to economize.

Off to see Peggy Gem.

Piggy Gem, the liar.

Writers: Come read me your work. Like a hooker soliciting customers.

I'll send her a poem. Request an audience with her. Pretend I'm a student, like one of those boys she's been meeting in parks.

Or I can pretend to know nothing. Spend a few nights at her apartment. And write her a letter:

> *Gem, this is what I learned while doing Hewitt's genealogical research: 1) It takes just six generations for a family tree to grow so large that, when printed as a chart, its branches can cover a*

huge table. 2) Charts that cover whole tables are like disposable tablecloths in a cheap restaurant. 3) A family wiped out by a storm becomes an uprooted family tree. 4) A branch without children offers no summer shade. 5) Eventually, the whole thing becomes firewood.

Enough botanical metaphors, Gem? I can read them as verses, if you like. I can fill several pages. Reed *has* been writing, after all.

The café across the street from her building is nearly empty. I sit and wait. *The Waiter*—the story of a man who is rewarded for his patience after waiting a lifetime for a wish to come true. Faith-based waiting.

I am more like a jealous husband, though, waiting for his cheating wife. Or the private investigator hired by the jealous husband to catch her in the act.

The world is full of waiters. Everyone waits. The serial killer. The thief. The clueless. The assassin. The avenger.

I don't qualify as an avenger. There are no retaliatory feelings in me against Gem. I'm just waiting.

Writing and waiting.

Unknotting the Soul: How to Get Rid of Your Enemies. The book's not what it seems. The words "How to Get Rid of..." attract the buyer. But there's no violence in the text. Siesta's idea is to tell the reader to "nurse a grudge," which is not the same as to hold a grudge. The grudge is the enemy, and we can nurse it by repeating our thoughts about it again and again—just like One-With-Time trips to the refrigerator: *Gem did that to me and I'm going to get her for it. Gem did that to me and I'm going to get her for it.*

Let the sentence become meaningless through repetition.

Gem did that to me and I'm going to get her for it. Gem did that to me and I'm going to get her for it.

Get rid of your enemies by kneading that fetid dough of vindictiveness in the far reaches of your brain. Knead those dark feelings until they dissolve into aromatic buns of freshly baked harmony.

Corny self-help trope sells books like hot cakes.

In minutes, I take my Gem buns out of the oven and I'm ready to call her—the phone call I've postponed far too long.

Ring. Ring.

Gem? Reed here.

Numerous pleasantries. She's happy to hear from me.

I ask if she's talked to Hewitt lately.

No. She hasn't even heard from him by email.

"Where are you, Reed."

In Galway, of course. In some boarding house without a name and no phone.

"Have you been writing?"

I don't answer that. Not a question to ask a man who's artistically menopaused, Gem.

"I'm going to Dublin to follow some genealogical leads."

She doesn't want me in Dublin. "Wait a couple of weeks, Reed. I'm too busy right now."

Busy listening to her newspaper-ad lovers. Busy reading their prose. "As a matter of fact, I *have* been writing," I say. "Would you like to compare notes, read our literary fruits to each other?"

She agrees but must schedule the meeting. Two weeks from now. And I can't stay in her apartment. We must meet at the café across the street from her building, she says. Do I remember its name?

I don't push it. The two weeks will give me the opportunity to map out her life in Dublin to the last detail. She's my new subject of research. The topic for another self-help book: *Vetting Your Sweetheart: How to Make Sure Your Fiancé(e) is Legit.* His and Hers editions. On the back cover: "Divorce rates will plummet with this handy bestseller." Chapters 3 and 4 teach the reader how to surreptitiously follow their spouse-to-be around town, how to interpret their subject's body language as they interact with strangers who are, in reality, actors hired by the reader.

The moment I put the receiver back in the cradle, I see Hewitt walking out of Gem's building.

Byron A. Hewitt. The horny old man. Doing his thing in Dublin.

Gem failed the vetting before it even started.

I knock on her door.

She lets me in without a word.

Yes, I tele-transported myself to Dublin. We both know we lied to each other just minutes ago.

Mutual deceit: a great conversation starter.

"Is he coming back?"

She shakes her head. "On his way to China."

I sit on the leather sofa and look around.

The Liars' Den: Group Therapy for Mendacious Minds.

There seems to be no aspiring writer hiding in her bedroom.

"You go first," I say.

"Where do you want me to start?"

"Here. Now."

"The bananas are laced," she says.

I look at a bunch of them sitting on the kitchen counter.

"They're part of the work you and I are doing."

I never heard of researchers playing the role of lab rats, especially without their knowledge.

She asks me to think of the bananas as a nicotine patch. "If you want to quit smoking, you wear the patch. If you want to stop wasting your life as an unimaginative writer, you eat the bananas."

"DNA-patched bananas? Laced with the cloned cells of a favorite writer? Terry Joyce's semen?"

"It's not that simple, Reed. Genes are not that important."

It's the hormones and proteins they produce, she says, that do most of the work. If you are not a good writer, it's because your WR125 gene is not producing the right protein.

"Think of the gene as a boss you've hired to run your brain as an efficient literary factory. His job is to tell the appropriate cells to produce the creative protein. But if it turns out you hired a lemon..."

Defective bosses make poor leaders, Gem says. So I must convince my Board of Directors to fire my WR125. Through tasty bananas, I bring in a new boss, one hopefully equipped with the right set of instructions.

Gem's only fear is that the bananas' WR125 might become too bossy. "It may move up the hierarchy—without permission—from the brain's literary factory to some other location in the corporation. It may give itself a promotion and put itself in charge of producing massive hair follicles on your tongue, for example, or some other undesirable byproduct of protein malfunction."

Reed the DNA receptacle. The guinea human.

A DNA-patch has to be administered gradually, in multiple exposures. The science is not fully developed yet. Lots of trial and error involved. Gem has been carefully documenting the process.

"There's no hair on my tongue yet."

"You're not the only one," she says.

She's been feeding bananas to all those failed writers who answered her ads. There are hundreds of writing genes being used in the program. Beckett, Wilde, Shaw—and those are only the born

Irish. Gem's in charge of all Europe. That explains her absences. The numerous trips to Paris. "We've been having a difficult time with the European Hemingways," she says.

"Too much fishing?" I ask. "Not enough hunting?"

"No. Suicide."

"Oh. Joyce didn't commit suicide, did he?"

She shakes her head.

"Good."

"You've never read Joyce?"

"Who has time to read fiction?"

"You don't know anything about him?"

"I don't want to read my biography before I've done what it says I did."

"Joyce was monogamous," Gem says. "Uxorious."

"Sorry, Gem. I don't know big Irish words."

"He idolized his wife."

Maybe this is Gem's way of vetting me for a husband. She watches my reaction to *uxorious*. She can see it in my eyes if I'm a spousal idolater or not.

"Joyce was crazy about things Scandinavian. He was litigious. Had terrible health problems with his eyes and teeth."

I feel a sudden pang under one of my molars. Gem the witch doctor, sticking needles in her Joyce-cloned Reed doll.

"He died of a perforated ulcer."

Ouch. My stomach.

"He was a steady economic parasite, and an unbearably self-centered human being. Many of his friends became ex-friends who took to calling him James Jesus Joyce."

Did he have any experience reaming toilets?

"He was unable to accept bad news," Gem adds. "Can you?"

"What can be worse than knowing I'll go blind, lose my teeth and die of a perforated ulcer?"

"You're just being ignorant, Reed. Genes don't work that way. The fact is, we don't have a clue how they work. That's why I joined Byron in all these experiments."

Every experiment needs guinea pigs.

There's one, Byron! Sitting at Le Clochard!

It was all a setup. Gem and Hewitt out on fishing expeditions, looking for failed writers drinking to their lack of success.

Coffee and beer for the hopeless.

Hard liquor for the more creatively destructive.

Bars. Cafés. University cafeterias.

Gem was the bait.

When they tired of cafés and bars, they turned to the classifieds.

"We've been looking for natural writers," she says. "Merely encouraging their genotypes with laced bananas."

"Byron must be exceedingly wealthy. At ten thousand dollars a month..."

"No. There are different pay scales," Gem says. "You were the only privileged one. The others live practically on nothing. Byron wanted to see how money affected the writing gene. If you allow a writer to live free from having to cook, keep house, or worry about expenses, can he become a better, more productive writer?"

With me, it failed. I didn't write a thing during fat cow. I only got ideas. Ideas aren't worth much. Everyone has them. They're just brain cells ruminating the intellectual cud, the useless parachutes that, once manufactured, never open.

"That's what the money was for—to see if, with all that freedom, the gene implants would kick in."

They didn't.

Other writers, the less-pampered guinea humans who struggled with dishwasher jobs they couldn't quit, did much better. The hope of getting published kept them going.

Gem says I can forget about another five thousand. Things are getting difficult for Hewitt in the States. He's on his way to China to negotiate additional research opportunities. The Chinese are significantly more open-minded when it comes to cloning and other types of genetic manipulation.

My job is effectively over.

Repeat it all again, Gem, so I can get used to the idea. Tell me you lied. Nurse me the truth like I've nursed my grudges.

"I lied to you," she says.

Gem the Disco Queen was an act.

Her bipolar episode: a performance, meant to discourage any romantic notions on my part.

No emotional relationships with the lab rats!

"Are you one of those non-swimmers," Gem asks, "who spend their lives seeking the intellectually shallow part of the pool?"

I go to the counter and take one of the bananas. Peel it. Start eating.

"Good," she says.

"Are you, Gem…one of those swimmers?"

She shakes her head. Takes a bite, too. The room is quiet while we chew.

"It's not just a matter of swimming, Gem, but also of changing your bathing suit. What's the use in swimming the seas of the world if you wear the same piece of Lycra every time your body gets wet?"

"You like to use metaphors, don't you?"

"I like to change bathing suits, and I *have* been writing."

She hands what's left of the banana to me. "Some modernists claim they can teach anyone to be a great writer. Byron doesn't agree, so he set out to prove it with WR125—in secret. He won't publish until his theory is proven."

I stand and walk around the apartment. Beautiful furniture from a Scandinavian catalog.

The guestroom is ready for me.

The kitchen is so clean, the sink and stove look new. The bananas on the counter are the only sign of food. *Food.*

"Are you angry?" she asks.

I go on with my tour.

Her bedroom: Clean laundry folded on her bed. White, sleeveless shirts and peach panties.

"Why did Byron choose me?"

"We did research. Traced your line back to Ireland…to a Joyce."

Wonderful. Like finding out I'm adopted. Born to blue-blood aristocrats, but raised by middle-class nurturers whose only dream involved a law degree and a six-figure mortgage. "Look at him," my mother used to say to my father. "Little Reed *likes* to argue. He's a shoo-in for a lawyer."

"Your Joyce gene goes way back," Gem says. She and Hewitt figured there might be something there.

"What am I supposed to do now?"

Gem raises her eyebrows. "Write."

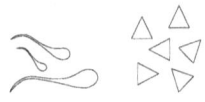

Suddenly, there's a role I must play: Gem's artistic houseguest. When the phone rings, she says I must answer "Gem Bishop's residence," with a phony South African accent. *Yes*—I should tell callers who ask—*I'm her houseguest, making a stop here as I go round the world collecting data for a monumental Marco Polo biography. Yes, I am writing it, too. I'm a historian and scientist, and discovered through my research that Marco Polo and Alexander the Great are related. The 1,600 years between them mean nothing in evolutionary terms. I'm also one of their descendants, I found out. And Gem—yes, I met her through the classifieds. I'm a clear example of how success can come to any writer who answers her ads.*

That's what I say to the aspiring writers who haven't met her yet. They call with their tiny voices, inquiring about the status of their applications. You have to apply and get in line to read to Gem these days.

Even when they're not here reading to Gem, the idea of their existence keeps me from concentrating on the blank page sitting on my desk, next to the rows of biology and chemistry books that Gem keeps in the guestroom.

She's out meeting new writers at some park most of the day. I've been here a week, and Hewitt already knows about it. If he and Gem are lovers, I don't want to know. I'll find out when he returns. And if it's true—and I find out—I don't want to know, either.

**

Another cigarette when the page is still blank and Gem gets home with one of her writers. A young woman. A pretty one who writes "Women's Liberation Poetry." An immigrant. Farsi. Her name is Delbar, and she says she came to Ireland to publish all the frustrations women can't express in her country. Her poetry turns out to be a step above reaming prison toilets with your fingernails, but not a very big step.

Gem's polite about it.

Hewitt Publishing doesn't do poetry, I want to tell Delbar, but we're stuck with her through her very long poem.

"Dagger of my pride to stab all testicles."

She calls men *testicles*, and she has no literary blood in her, just anger. "The testicles," she reads, "wage war on women, like storms buffeting a gentle sapling."

I open a banana.

"Two tiny marbles in a rotten sack—the pitiful symbol behind testicular hegemony over women."

I've never heard verses this long.

"So hear this, sisters. Hear my call..."

Gem and I laugh when the phone rings in reply to Delbar's command.

It's Hewitt. He's in a cab on his way here from the airport.

We ask the poetess to leave a copy of her poem for consideration. Gem had been thinking of a female Nobel Laureate in Farsi. But for Delbar, the testicles stand in the way.

Hewitt turns down the banana I bring to him on a plate. He's a whirlwind. Too high on caffeine to bother with food or sleep. Doesn't even want the guestroom. "The couch's fine."

The news from America is that a Congressional Commission has been formed to investigate "alleged genetic experiments on humans by one Doctor Byron A. Hewitt." The "Irish Mengele," they're calling him now. And here he is, in front of me, speaking in accents I've never heard him intone.

He's Irish.

Gem knew this, of course. She's been an insider all along. With the rest of us, Hewitt used his phony American accent just like I use my phony South African—to keep people at bay.

"When you talk to people in a fake accent," Hewitt says, "you don't take them seriously. They don't become your friends." His thick, curly hair—no longer in a ponytail—looks as good as ever. The result of genetic manipulation?

On the television, a spokesman for the congressional beagles in Washington explains they will get to the bottom of this, whatever it takes.

"Prudish America," Hewitt says. "Sensationalist America, where headlines convict you without a shred of evidence. All of their papers have activists hiding behind every headline."

Irish "Doctor" to Stand Trial for Frankengenes.

I look at Gem and, for some reason, think of Joan of Arc, who was accused of being a witch by the medieval equivalent of headlines. But was she really a witch? Maybe there was, after all, a hidden motive behind Joan's trial, and her enemies burned her for ulterior motives. Her sexuality, perhaps?

To remedy that historical wrong, a new scholarly bestseller by author Reed Lodge can uncover the truth behind Joan's pyre:

Outing Joan of Arc: Homophobia in Fifteenth Century France.

A bestseller as full of activism as any headline.

Volume Two: *Flaming the Heroine: Joan of Arc's Real Crime.*

Why can't I write it?

**

At three in the morning, Hewitt's still talking. The television is off. The tone is subdued. With his America-bashing session over, he's telling me about his upcoming publishing empire, one based on science books alone. He wants people to stop reading fiction. Science, he says, is the only path to true insight. We must learn everything we can about our universe. And science books are the answer.

"Joyce's gene, Hemingway's gene, Proust's gene—they're simply not going to work, Reed, other than to make the gene recipients compulsively bad writers. And that's exactly my point. We have to flood the market with trashy novels. Turn readers off fiction by destroying the novel, just like Joyce did. Every pseudo-intellectual claims to admire Joyce, but Joyce wasn't writing when he wrote *Finnegans*. He was laughing his bloody cacks off. His *corpse* is still laughing."

I am tired and need to go to bed, please.

"*Ooes@z^l'skei*. What did I say?" Hewitt asks.

I'm too sleepy. Gem's in her room, in her bed. Siesta's waiting in mine. Let me go.

"*Ooes@z^l'skei* means nothing," he answers himself. "It's incomprehensible. Why? Because I'm paraphrasing Joyce. The problem is, Joyce didn't finish the job." Hewitt stares at me, as if I were the chosen one to do so. "Someone has to annihilate the novel once and for all, Reed. It's an obsolete form of communication."

Hewitt says he'll soon teach a creative-writing course in Scotland. "The type of course frequented by dolts who swear inspiration can be learned."

I think I've figured Hewitt out. He's a kindred spirit. A jack of all trades. Joyce's gene was meant to make him zillions from publishing literary masterpieces. It didn't work, so he's on to something else.

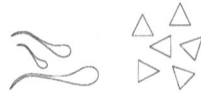

Gem and I follow the televised congressional hearings like new-lyweds on a permanent honeymoon. Shared bliss without the sex.

Contrary to what the headlines said earlier, Hewitt is not on trial. For now, he's only testifying before Congress. And he's giving the senators an earful, taking every opportunity to insult them.

"You boys are falling asleep at the scientific wheel," he says. "By accepting the orthodoxy that human chromosomes are full of junk DNA, you play the same role as an illiterate man who calls books 'wasted paper' just because *he* can't read them. So we're not talking tits on a bull here. *Junk* DNA is not the useless mass that clueless biologists like to tell you it is. We have to learn how to read it, Mr. Chairman. If we don't know the language, then we must experiment in order to learn it. *Experimentation*—that's the key word. Without genetic experimentation, it won't be America but China that will know the intricacies of what makes us tick. American brainpower is now flying west, over the Pacific, to create the new America, the America of the twenty-first century. It's called China. That's what you'll get if you don't take off your phony ethical hats. So stop being so damned moral, and allow science to progress."

"He's going to finish the hour with the Bad Liver speech," Gem says. She wrote it for him. She knows every word.

Hewitt asks the esteemed senators whether any of them has had a liver transplant.

No takers.

"You're lucky," he says. "Five thousand Americans had one last year. Geneticists are scrambling for stem cells to grow pig livers to use in yet more transplants, thus increasing the number of recipients tenfold. If you ask me, it's an absolutely pigheaded approach."

The senators laugh and congratulate themselves for still having a sense of humor.

"My research," Hewitt goes on, "transcends the surgeon. There's no such thing as a bad liver, gentlemen. No such thing as the need for a transplant. All we have to do is guide the hyper-regeneration of liver cells. In an accelerated process, two months of therapy will yield you a brand new liver without the use of a scalpel."

Gem wipes a tear from her face. I realize there's a lot more than science invested in this, and I'm just an observer.

The cameras follow Hewitt out to a sea of reporters, digital recorders, and more cameras. First question: *When are you going to go back to your cloning work?*

"It's hormones, not cloning," Hewitt explains patiently. He looks like an angel being harassed by thousands of devils, a lone white blood cell suffocated by millions of red ones. The questions come at him like strobes: *Did you test the hormones on yourself first? How many victims did you hire to experiment on? Haven't you made enough money? Do you like playing God?*

His patience doesn't last. "You ignoramus paperboys," he says. "Moron journalists who don't know the first thing about science. That's why this country's going to hell, with all the little feckers like ya, all shitting on one's quest for knowledge."

The mass media retaliate.

Irish Mengele Loses His Temper.

Out come the investigative reporters.

Hewitt Didn't Have U.S. Visa. Lived Here Illegally.

Dig. Dig. Dig.

Hewitt's Ex-Wife: "He Experimented on Me, Without Me Bloody Knowledge!"

Tabloid America is fascinated. People want blood.

And they get it.

Judge Orders Mad Scientist's Arrest.

Charged in connection to a "Hemingway gene-cloning experiment," the television says.

Now that the impending trial has really put him in the public eye, even evolutionary biologists take turns ridiculing the Irish Rogue. His efforts are "a monumental waste of money on dangerous, Hitlerian experiments," one says. "Practicing science without a soul."

Ethical questions pile up. Hewitt's medical license is revoked. A former cleaning lady is brought in for a sworn affidavit. She's "deeply religious," the papers say. She saw what Hewitt was up to and piously stole several of his research notebooks. The Center for Disease Control pored over every page, every annotation. The charge: "Dangerous experiments with frankengenes."

Crimes against humanity.

Lock him up.

Gem spends one, two, maybe three days in her bedroom. To her, I don't exist—until she comes out and asks me to get her something to eat. Bread and canned soup from a nearby mini-market, where

I'm aware of eyes staring at me as I make my purchase. There's an unusual number of police vans around Temple Bar these days.

The soup is too hot when I serve it, so she sulks while she waits, saying it's all over—the Project, years of study, and the future of biology itself.

"You can always do something else, Gem. Start by repeating this to yourself: 'I don't have to be a biologist all my life. I can be more. I can be more. I can be more.' It's a mantra you can turn into prayer. I practice it as a religion myself. I can be a lumberjack, an economist, an engineer, a politician..."

"Then why aren't you—any of those things—if you claim to have the time?"

I look at the clock on the kitchen counter. In the seconds it takes a tree to fall in slow motion, I ask my many selves the same question. Reed the lumberjack: Why aren't you communing with trees? Reed the economist: Why aren't you dictating market policy? Mr. engineer: Why aren't you designing power plants? And why aren't you, the politician, getting elected?

"You never finish anything you start," Gem says.

"I can't. It's my religion."

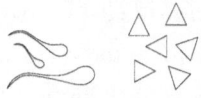

Online headlines from Washington: *Irish Rogue Flees American Justice.* Hewitt gives an interview from his home in Beijing. "I'm not a fugitive and I'm not in hiding." He will fight any efforts to extradite him. He's confident, he says, that Chinese common sense and love of science will prevail over America's troglodyte sense of ethics.

First day of the month now. No five thousand for me, but enough for Gem to keep us, and the Project, afloat.

As long as the media don't find us, Gem insists, we'll keep on gathering data—finishing what we started. I no longer have to participate as a lab rat if I don't want to. I've been promoted. Any ethical qualms? Get out.

My idea is to start writing Hewitt's biography. Shed some true light on the man before he grows jaundiced from yellow journalism. I ask Gem whether I can use her diaries for input.

"What diaries?" She doesn't keep one. Security reasons.

I confess I read one in Zurich.

"Those were notes for a novel." She's not even upset I violated her privacy. *The Secret Life of Madame Curie*, the novel is called. Gem finished it, like she does everything she starts, and will soon start looking for an agent.

"Can I read it?"

"No. It's in Byron's apartment in Paris."

"He has property in Paris?"

"Of course. He has homes in Vienna, Glasgow, Beijing, Figueira da Foz..."

Money's no object. The papers say Hewitt charges two hundred thousand dollars per *exclusive* interview these days. Hungry media empires pay the required amount, despite their protestations that *exclusive* should mean exclusive for at least a month, instead of a day.

The world is following Hewitt like it followed Lindbergh on his first solo flight across the Atlantic—with the half-wish that he crash in mid-flight and make even better news fodder. Collective grief is the best excuse for gloating.

Hewitt loves the attention. Fifteen minutes of fame turned into hours of opportunity to expose the world to his science. "Cloning is useless to humans already conceived," he tells one reporter. "Everyone talks about how it takes seven years for the human body to replace all its cells. But not all cells are replaceable. My goal, then, is to not only make it possible to regenerate *every* cell in the human body, but also to genetically guide all aspects of that regeneration."

Every evening, Hewitt looks at the camera and speaks to his world audience: "You decide. In seven years, you may want to be so-and-so, or have such-and-such. An athlete. A true blonde. A boxer. A writer. It *can* be done. All it takes is seven years."

Nobel Prize material, supporters say.

The Seven-Year Switch, detractors laugh.

In the end, it doesn't really matter. A few days later, no one's paying Hewitt any attention. There are terrorist bombs to report. Airplane disasters. Train derailments. Civil wars. Famines. And a serial-killing English nanny making the rounds in French Canada. Hewitt scrambles to compete, like a fading movie star trying anything to restart his career. He yells. He shouts. He screams. But spent movie icons come back only when they're dead.

The cameras are gone.

The microphones are deaf.

On a Tuesday morning, we hear that Hewitt's been arrested in Tianjin and extradited to the U.S. The Chinese couldn't defy Uncle Sam. Uncle knows how to use his international tools of diplomacy: The World Bank. Foreign investment. Preferred-country status for trade. Chinese goods flowing into America. Panda bears. Fugitives.

What America wants, America gets.

There's a video camera next to a bunch of rotting bananas on the kitchen counter. I take it and start recording. Mouse droppings on the lime-green laminate. In extreme close-up, they look like charred sausages.

I move around the room.

There's Gem on the couch. She stares at the camera. "What are you doing?"

"I've always wanted to be a film director. Did you ever dream of being a movie star?"

"I can't act," she says.

"Play yourself. Take a break from biology."

She's not paying attention. Her mind's on the news. I pan to capture the TV screen. It's a live report on an imminent raid on "Byron Hewitt's clandestine lab in Dublin." They're showing our street. Our building. Our windows. I walk to the nearest window and point the camera down, to a crowd of news manufacturers looking up from the street—our cameras staring at each other.

On the television, troops are shown mobilizing. A photo of Hewitt follows. "His accomplices," the anchor says, "are believed to be preparing a bio-terror attack with genetically-modified viruses, operating out of *this* building."

Again, our windows.

Gem tells me to fill the tub with hot water.

"We're making a soup," she says.

I dump all the test tubes' contents into the cauldron. Add a pinch of bath salts, DNA kits, notebook computers, and video camera.

On the TV screen: a close-up of shiny black boots. Storm troopers storming up the building's stairs.

"Pull the computers out," Gem says. "Place them on the electromagnet."

I turn the magnet on. It's like a powerful vacuum sucking data from the hard drives.

There's knocking on the apartment next door. We can see the gloved knuckles on TV.

"Police!"

So far, they have the wrong place.

I have the shower running. The bathroom's full of steam. A tropical rain forest on a primordial pond.

Next door, the shiny black boots are stomping. And Gem yells, "Pull the stopper!"

Drain the soup.

"They get nothing."

She doesn't know I've kept two test tubes in my pocket.

The television says the FBI and Interpol have rounded up writers all across Europe and America. Our Hemingways in Paris. Our Zweigs in Vienna. Tolstoys in Saint Petersburg. All in custody and being questioned.

Gem the cleaning woman, pouring potions down the toilet. Burning her notes. "Anything they find," she says, "they'll use against Byron—and us."

The storm troopers are coming. The gene police, with their batons and riot gear. I don't want to see their faces, so I turn off the TV and check the basket on the kitchen counter. It contains several sets of keys in beautiful key holders with handwritten labels. *Paris. Vienna. Figueira. London.* Where do I go?

"They're here," Gem says, and just stands there, waiting for the door to fly off its hinges.

I can't do that. I pretend there's a fire, one bigger than the one in the bathroom's tin trashcan, where her former research notes smolder. "Fire! Fire!"

I give her a kiss on the fourth hair of her right eyebrow.

Good bye.

Me and Siesta—we make our escape through the bedroom window. Me and Siesta, with a bag full of cash and two test tubes in my pocket.

Genius: The Life & Times of Byron A. Hewitt. "The outstanding biography by Reed Lodge, the fugitive and former assistant researcher of Irish roots."

"Excellently narrated by the guinea human who's well on his way to becoming the star author of Dr. Hewitt's media empire."

"Author Reed Lodge has created a masterpiece. Never mind he's at large."

three

When I go on trips, I always leave home with the thought that I may not return. Point A may never be Point A again. And that's fine. The important thing is the arrival. Point B. Portuguese sun. Figueira da Foz, where the men are strong and the women don't care.

Hewitt's penthouse near Picadeiro features several waterbeds and four bathrooms with sauna stalls and whirlpools. They say a biographer must experience the same lifestyle as his subject in order to write an accurate bio. I'm all for that. And pity the bloke who pens the life of Mother Teresa.

Volume One of the biography will describe Project Shakespeare and its triumphs. Hewitt's trial will have to wait for Volume Two. It's not a good idea to jinx the outcome of a trial by writing about it before there's a verdict. That's how city officials give the evil eye to a politician when they name a street after him while he's still alive. Soon after the new street signs are up, the politician either drops dead or loses his marbles.

I don't know if my name's in the news anymore. I don't know what happened to Gem, the other writers, or Hewitt. When the news is bad, it's better to tune out and ignore it. I've stored all of Hewitt's television sets in a closet. When I go out, I avert my eyes at the sight of every newsstand.

Maybe my photograph is making the rounds. *Reed: International suspect. Collaborator. Literary terrorist.*

When I go out for groceries, I pick up a pair of sunglasses, and come right back.

On the terrace above the penthouse, I strip and take daily sunbaths in preparation for anonymous trips to the beach. No one will recognize me tanned, in a tight bathing suit, sunglasses, and shortly cropped hair.

Siesta is bored to death with the sunbathing routine. I reek of fake coconut oil, she says. But I tell her: Be patient. Let our brains formulate. Enjoy our fabulous surroundings.

I serve myself a tall glass of water, with ice.

The kitchen is spotless, except for a few mouse turds on the lime-green counter.

I take a shower.

Water inside, water outside. They used to recommend it to those who wanted to quit smoking. Feel like a cigarette? Take a shower. Drink a gallon of water. Don't let the craving overcome you.

I try the water treatment, but it doesn't work very well when what you're craving is normality. Living with your pillow in a two-million-dollar penthouse without any human contact isn't normal. I'm sure that's how Terminex must have felt in his rodent condo on Cheese Boulevard. I saved him from the damaging comforts of his pampered, pet-store existence. And like him, I need help migrating from this luxury to the insides of some wall, where I can fight the rodents that are shredding my self-confidence.

I'm not imagining things, Siesta. The laced bananas have had no effect on me. If Joyce's gene were truly lodged in my brain, I'd be sitting all day in the living room—ignoring your yelling for attention—and writing a monumental masterpiece of supreme linguistic virtuosity, filled with words that "elbow their way on to the page," as literary critics might say, and "explode there with the significance of multiple orgasms."

But No. It didn't work, Hewitt. Project Shakespeare was a resounding failure. I feel more like singing than writing. I sing during my two-hour showers. Tenor in the artificial rain. I sing while making love to the sun on the terrace. Portuguese love songs from your CD collection. I sing like there's no tomorrow.

Another tall glass of water to soothe my singer's vocal chords. Cities like Paris, London and Dublin go through fifty-zillion gallons of water a day. All those singers and orators in need of a drink.

Without water, the possibilities are endless: World War III. The Water Shortage War. Hydroless Armageddon. This is where Hewitt would come in with his genetic research, developing a water-retention gene. Humans as hydro-blobs: CamelHumans®, the new breed that won't need to go to war over water.

Failing the development of such a gene, we have to do something about water. Siesta says the world is running out of it. Too many people using too much. The only solution: Recycle the liquid through new treatment plants that can, in two hours flat, turn what you flush down your toilet into an elixir from your kitchen tap. I know what she's talking about because I did the work once—had the job for only two weeks, but long enough to learn much about water.

The powers that be don't want you to know anything about how sewage and water treatments work. You just flush your toilet, and let the pompous Water Engineers do the rest.

Jacks of all trades aren't so easily turned away, though. We *must* know how the process works. And when we learn it, we find that there's nothing to it. It's not a science, after all, just a series of filtering steps.

The sunscreen bottle doesn't want me to squeeze her anymore. She screams when she's empty. I have to go out for more, and a sandwich, and a drink, and more water.

The outing requires a long starvation walk—Picadeiro, Avenida do Brasil, Silva Guimarães—and a table at my favorite restaurant, where the owner's beautiful daughter serves me the sandwich with an empty glass and a bottle of water. Just to make conversation, I ask her not to open the bottle and, instead, fill my glass with tap water. She doesn't care—not interested in skinny, suntanned weir-does wearing sunglasses while eating their sandwiches. As if to spite me, she slams the full glass on the table, and I see some orange particles suspended in the liquid. *Particulate matter.*

Something's definitely wrong with the water-treatment process here. They probably can't afford the alum, so they have poor *flocculation* leading to defective *sedimentation.* These are the big words dreamed up by the water-treatment boys so the public stays in the dark about the process. *Raw water. Protozoal contamination. Finished water. Coliforms. Mutagens. Monochloramines.* They just pile up the terminology. "Shut up and let the experts handle it," they tell the rest of the world.

But I refuse. We the commoners can do a better job turning this town's sewage into the elixir of life. I can do it on Hewitt's terrace with a couple of cement tanks filled with algae.

How to Build Your Own Sewage-Treatment Plant.

Chapter 10: "Pump the toilet's products to the first tank. Let the algae eat the scum. Pretend it's a fish tank in your living room. Use a separate pump to transfer the primary-treated water from Tank One to Tank Two. And—*voilà!*—an alternative to bottled water."

Reed, the water-treatment guru, giving book talks everywhere. Hundreds of bookstores visited. Thousands of books signed with his special, organic, squid-ink pen.

The beautiful daughter is on the phone, talking with her arms. She will soon meet the man of her dreams, marry him, and have beautiful children. Portugal will thank her. Life will go on.

But what heights would Portugal reach if all of her ten babies turned out like James Joyce? What would such a writer do to his motherland if he were an army of thousands instead of only one man?

Water is the answer.

Water and test tubes.

On my way back to the penthouse, Dr. Hurt's bestsellers glare at me from a bookstore's window. Translated into Portuguese. *O Exile do Papa*, by Wallace Hur, son-of-a-pen writer. *O Explorador do Quintal.* The Backyard Explorer. *O Deus é Elétrico.* God is Electric. *Papa Sam.* No translation required. Dr. Hurt looks thirty years younger on the back covers of his books. Youth and beauty purchased with what he's earned writing my stories. I am trying to translate what a blurb says, but someone outside keeps on yelling, *Polícias! Polícias!*

I rush home with my new bottle of sunscreen and see that, indeed, there are a few too many police vans in the neighborhood. There's also a note stuck to Hewitt's door. It's in Portuguese and in cursive. I can't read either one and leave it there so nobody thinks I'm home.

I keep the lights out in the entrance hallway. Close all the curtains. I can barely see the walls and the prints of marine fantasies covering them—those funny little men catching big fish with harpoons that look like toothpicks.

On the penthouse terrace, Siesta is being ravished by the sun, as she likes to say. I strip again, and with my thoroughly tanned birthday suit, I look over the edge of the abyss and see dozens of police officers walking their dogs on the street.

They're sniffing my footprints.

The officers say I'm ninety-two years old, and a dangerous foreigner.

I get dressed. Silk shirt, half open. Gold chain on my tanned chest.

Ninety-two.

It's the age when the neighbors start thinking, if not saying, *He's lived long enough. Could die at any moment. Better get all the oral history out of him before he expires.*

And so they're after me, with their police dogs and media retinues—radio and television crews wishing to record my every memory.

"I don't have any!" I yell at them. "All I remember is how to treat water, and that's what I'll do till the end of my days."

Figueira must use the Mondego River as its source of raw water. If I follow the contour of the river, northeast, to Coimbra, I should be able to find the municipal waterworks.

The taxi driver I hire claims not to know where they process the city's water. "*Esgoto, filtro, boca,*" I tell him through my English-Portuguese dictionary. But he's not very enterprising, won't make an effort to find out where I want to go.

More police dogs arrive. They're turning downtown into a kennel, so I have to compromise. "Alright, take me to Coimbra."

He starts driving and says it will cost a great deal of money to ride a taxi up there. I'd be better off taking the bus.

To shut him up, I hand him a fistful of euros. "Just drop me off near Coimbra, at some seafood restaurant as close to the river as possible."

Poor planning can force the most stubborn of activists to compromise. I'll have to forget the waterworks, then. At the restaurant, I'll go in the bathroom, pour a few drops from the test tubes into the toilet, and flush. Joyce's gene should be able to survive the ammonia feeders and chlorinators downriver. When the intake facility sucks in water to supply Figueira's main, the virus should be intact.

There are hundreds of thousands of novels out there that end with some religious fanatic poisoning the city's water supply as an act of terrorism. Bestsellers, most of them. The Mondego River in Figueira. The Liffey in Dublin. The Corrib in Galway. The Potomac. Mississippi. Amazon. Zambezi. "River Vengeance," they call it. *Religious Retribution.* "You contaminate mine, I contaminate yours."

But this is not terrorism, just RiverRun, "from swerve of shore to bend of bay," as James Joyce has put it.

> **RiverRun** / *rívêrrun* / n. **1** clear sludge, fit for human consumption. **2** a proven method of intellectual dissemination, collective gene therapy, and literary pollination. **3** a strictly benevolent form of terrorism, propagated by Johnny Apple Reed as he travels the world with Gem's tubes in his pocket.

In Paris, the Seine receives Hemingway and Becket. In London, the Thames gets Orwell, Austen, Dickens and Defoe. Just a few drops left of the stuff in my pocket. Zweig for the Danube in Vienna. Koestler joins him downstream in Budapest. And Havel swims in the Vltava in a velvet swimming suit.

Reed, the benevolent terrorist.

And when the tubes are empty, Siesta asks me, very innocently, "How many nuns does it take to save a soul?" It's like one of those ethnic jokes that ask how many &@$!#% it takes to screw in a light bulb.

I don't know, Siesta, and I don't want to know. Ninety-two-year-old bags of bones don't like to offend anybody.

"Here's a clue: The answer involves bananas."

Shut up, Siesta, and pass me the word salad.

"Come on, Reed," she insists. "How many banana-eating *nuns*?"

Damn it, Siesta! Let me piss my pants in peace! Let me slam the fridge door in harmony, and take a slash, and one more time now: sssssSLAM! SLAM! SLAM! There go the hinges. Look at them go, Siesta! It's the Portuguese *polícias* swarming the place, coming in their black Mariahs like ants riding a beetle to a bloody picnic. A baubleclass and waldalure-ringring-kind-of-thing, at all hours of the pissing day, when Heuston marketh Hurt and the men just stand there with their groin conditions, so full of their bitch bags waiting for the nasty obituarist to do her thing. "Take that!" she'll write about them, "You Darwineous dead gimps, with boxes for bollocks and macho nothing-nothings tucked in your brains, you piss-and-water DNA-experimenters, survival-of-the-fleeting fittest youse. When you finally sit down at my dinner table for your last supper, and I'm more than ready to write your nasty obituaries, you'll bring me cocktails with sandpaper napkins and laced olives bubbling in calamari-ink wine. That's right. You'll be me servants, and dead you will be, as dead as you are now!"

And only then—when piss finally turns into water—will we be able to accept our innumerable blessings.